THE OMEGA POINT

The Omega Point

George Zebrowski

NEW ENGLISH LIBRARY
TIMES MIRROR

To the first Clarion Writers Workshop . . . 1968

And Anne and Edward Krutol,
who helped make it possible for me to be there

First published in the United States of America by Ace Books, 1972

*

FIRST NEL PAPERBACK EDITION JULY 1974

*

NEL Books are published by
New English Library Limited from Barnard's Inn, Holborn, London E.C.1.
Made and printed in Great Britain by Hunt Barnard Printing Ltd., Aylesbury, Bucks.

45001804 0

Contents

About the Author:

GEORGE ZEBROWSKI'S short stories have appeared in *Worlds of If*, *The Magazine of Fantasy and Science Fiction*, *New Worlds Quarterly*, *Infinity*, and elsewhere. Born in 1945 in Villach, Austria of Polish parents, he grew up in England, Manhattan, Miami and The Bronx, believing from an early age that he was going to be a writer of science fiction. In 1969 he became editor of *The Bulletin of the Science Fiction Writers of America*. He has taught science fiction on the college level at SUNY-Binghampton, Harpur College, where he studied philosophy.

The Omega Point is his first novel.

1. Immortal Enemy

'What would we do without our enemies?'

– Teilhard de Chardin

'In his own unconscious every one of us is convinced of his own immortality.'

– Freud

Gorgias ran.

The three centuries of his life seemed only a moment to him, not nearly enough time to carry out his father's vow of vengeance against the earthborn peoples. In his heart a billion souls cried out for him to avenge their deaths and the home world's destruction. He had never seen the ruined planet New Anatolia in the Hercules Globular Cluster, but its ghost ruled his life, giving meaning to his future and binding together all the events of the past.

The shrill cries of his ancestors wearied him sometimes and he longed for the warmth of the orange-yellow sun of Myraa's World half a galaxy away, where he could gaze across the grassy plain in front of her hilltop house where she lived alone, safe from the domination of earthmen. He wished for the colors of a natural world to replace the sterile metallic innards of the whisper ship and the gray unsubstantiality of the warpscanner screen.

He stared at the four black smudges on the screen, the unmistakable signs of hunter ships following his wake in the vast unreality of hyperspace. He could tell they were not sure that he was ahead of them. Their only clue was the intermittent buckling of the space in front of them, but they could not be sure it was being caused by the presence of his whisper ship, or by some other vessel.

At their present rate they could not possibly close with him for another earth week, and by then he would be at his destination. If they should suddenly quicken their pace, he would still have enough time to outdistance their sensors.

He set the ship on automatic whisper drive. According to the time indicator under the screen panel it was now a hundred standard hours since his last sleep period. He got up from the command station and made his way aft to his small sleeping quarters.

Gorgias slept.

But the instant which marked his life became long: thirty decades, and he felt each year of scars, loneliness and waste, repeated endlessly across space-time. The void was a vast belly in which he wandered, a great abyss echoing his fears.

He cried into the echo, and the starlight came coldly into his eyes; and he saw the fearful figures of earthmen superimposed on the starfields, hunched over their glowing instruments in their ships, hating him and tracking, endlessly tracking....

He woke up hating.

* * *

The star showed as a black disk on the gray screen. It fluctuated in size from moment to moment, a distorted version of the real star in normal space. Gorgias set his exit coordinates and blinked into normal space-time, at once turning the black sun on like a light. He had intended to come out in the shadow of Wolfe IV, but the hunters were too far behind him to make any difference. They still did not seem to be really aware of him, or else they were assuming that he was going to come down on the planet where they would not be able to pinpoint his position.

He brought the ship down on the nightside of the earthlike world, knowing that the hunter ships would take up a position around the planet and wait for him to leave. He was ready to deal with that contingency. Meanwhile a remote position on the surface and the ship's sensor-absorption screen would insure that he would not be found. In space the sensor-absorption screen showed up as a discontinuity, but on the surface of a world it would merge the ship with the planetary mass, making it impossible to detect with conventional instruments. It was too easy to disappear on a planet, and for that reason he was sure the hunters would wait for him to leave.

The ocean was dark below him on the screen, the wrinkled surface of a viscous plain. The sky was overcast and the port city lights of New Bosporus glowed on the horizon against the massing clouds which would soon swallow sky and stars. He brought the ship in lower over the water and raced toward the city.

New Bosporus was a city of ten million Earth Federation citizenry on a planet supporting five alien humanoid nations with a total population of sixty million. Most of the land area was still frontier and the majority of the inhabitants chose to live in the coastal cities of the two major continents, one in the northern hemisphere and one in the southern. Two-thirds of the planet was water.

Gorgias slowed the ship's forward motion to a hover when it was a few miles from the beach and settled it into the water gently. A hundred feet below the surface he moved the ship forward to within a quarter mile of the shore, letting it settle into three hundred feet of water. The bottom was sandy and level, and the ship touched it with a bump and was still.

Gorgias sat back in his command seat and reviewed what he had learned during his brief visit to New Bosporus one earth year ago. Marko Ruggerio, earth's greatest composer, was in the city now to conduct the first performance of his newest work, a massive percussion cantata on ethical themes from the Earth-Herculean War. The performance was to be held in the great city auditorium, a quarter-mile high structure of transparent plastic and metal, complete with environmental controls and perfect acoustics.

Gorgias pushed a button on his right armrest panel. A voice spoke from the screen audio. It was a documentary talk which he had recorded a year ago, the prologue to an interview with Marko Ruggerio. Gorgias listened with amusement to the self important tones of the commentator.

'. . . and the Herculean Empire lasted for twelve hundred years, A.D. 5000–6200, in the open globular cluster M-13. The cluster contains more than 50,000 stars and is 34,000 light-years from the Federation capitol, Earth. The greatest concentration of stars is in the core, which is 30 light-years in diameter . . .'

Facts like these cannot be used for much, Gorgias thought: the distortions would come later.

'. . . the hybrid peoples of the empire were the result of crossbreeding between earth colonials, freed from the solar system by the early stardrives, and the original humanoids of the cluster. The resulting stock was very long-lived. Average height was five feet and a few inches, with a delicate frame and strong musculature, and dark hair. Individuals needed about one-third the normal sleep period required by native earthmen, due to a very different metabolic system . . .'

Gorgias could almost admire the way the commentator had slipped over the transition years, the time during which the hordes of arriving earthmen had butchered the native populations of a slightly backward empire, taking their women for wives and concubines against their will. There was no doubt that the earth colonials had been absorbed, but the lifeblood of the original peoples could not forget so easily.

'. . . many of the females exhibited telepathic powers.

The males were intelligent but very high-strung types; they gave evidence of empathic abilities, but seldom equalled the women in telepathic consistency . . . '

And it was the women, Gorgias knew, who had seen the horror in earthmen's minds at the end of the war and had spread the terror which had contributed to the final collapse.

'The planetary societies were invariably military. In 4900 Gorgias the First united twenty worlds in the cluster by sheer force of arms and a shrewd alliance of friends. By 5000 he had completely wiped out the original humanoids of the cluster, or had driven them into hiding on the remote worlds of the group, leaving only the hybrid, earth-derived forms . . . '

Lies. Gorgias the First had all but given his life to help drive out Federation interests and help restore something of the old culture. And he had succeeded, making it necessary to rewrite history in order to make him a criminal in Earth's eyes.

'Earth anthropologists who visited the empire during the following centuries came away with the impression that its people were mad, frantic workers chasing a future they would not live to see.

'Many historians now believe that the war began as a mistake, but the following reprisals were carried out with such fierce hatred of earthmen that when war was finally declared in 5148, earthmen were forced to adopt a strategy of extermination toward the Hurculean forces . . . '

No one ever asks, Gorgias thought, what Earth Federation bases and armed populations were doing in the Hercules Cluster to begin with, and why they did not leave when asked for more than a century.

' . . . and in battle it was impossible to take a Herculean alive. The few who were captured usually found a way to kill themselves and their guards in the most brutal ways . . . '

He wasn't going to mention the games earthies staged with their prisoners, humiliating them to the point of suicide and senseless fury.

'The war ended in 6200 with the total destruction of the empire, after three quiet spells lasting about fifty years each. Toward the end there were very few prisoners and many powerful renegades remained free, killing and looting settlements on the Federation's rim . . . '

Gorgias felt a surge of pride for those lonely survivors. He was the last one. . . .

'The greatest of these was Gorgias the Third and his son of the same name. He had been a young captain when the war ended, and he was never captured. Speculation has it that he was almost five hundred years old when he died in 6600. He left his resources and his spirit of resistance to his son, who is still at large and in possession of his father's Whisper Ship . . . '

Did he detect a bit of admiration in the commentator's voice? It was not possible to completely suppress the facts of true heroism, thought Gorgias.

' . . . Gorgias' son has been a thief, a saboteur, a political assassin and a general nuisance . . . '

And soon he was going to be a cultural assassin, striking at the very pride of the Earth Federation, by disrupting Marko Ruggerio's concert parody of the great war.

'Hunters go out every year, but with no success. Gorgias the Fourth is the last and most resourceful of the surviving renegades.

'Five thousand Herculeans survived the death of the empire. Their home worlds destroyed one by one, they fled to the frontier worlds in the cluster. Present day Herculeans are thinly scattered across fifty star systems, where they lead the lives of outcasts. A half-dozen popular names are used when referring to them. In reality they are quite harmless, busying themselves with a new religious cult which has its center on Myraa's World, named after a Herculean woman connected with the revival.

'Romantic legend has it that an army of Herculeans escaped into the smaller Magellanic Cloud, 170,000 light-years beyond the galactic rim, and still exists . . . '

Someday, Gorgias promised himself, he was going to go and find them. It would mean digging out the knowledge from his father's base to modify the ship to cover that distance as quickly as possible, but he was going to try.

'It would be an impossible task to go looking for them among all those stars; but even if it exists, how effective a military force could it be after so long? A few modern strategists insist, however, that Gorgias has a base somewhere from which he draws supplies. They believe there might be an arsenal there which could be very dangerous if he could raise an army; and by the same token, even a small surviving force in the Magellanic Cloud might do considerable damage if it comes equipped with some of the weapons of the empire.

'Gorgias' Whisper Ship, for example, is the last of the old weapons, a virtually indestructible vessel which is said to be linked to the brain pattern of the owner, and which destroys itself with terrible fury upon his death, or when the link is broken, presumably by excessive distance.

'There is no list or directory of all the older weapons, some of which are thought to date back to mid-empire, and this fact intrigues each new generation of military men and historians . . . '

Useless knowledge, thought Gorgias; they know quite a bit, but can do nothing with it.

' . . . one of the reasons originally given for the complete destruction of New Anatolia, the home world of the empire, is that it was the source of a frightening line of weaponry. The Herculean armorers and their factories had to be destroyed to shorten the war, and to prevent them from developing something which might have been decisive in their favor . . . '

Stalemate, Gorgias thought. The decisive weapon exists somewhere, but it had come too late to be used. He had been looking for it since his father's death; he had left him only a few clues, but he was sure they would be enough eventually.

'. . . and to date hunter ships have failed to capture Gorgias, although an amnesty has been offered many times, in an effort to gain control of the Whisper Ship. Gorgias has not responded.'

And I never will, you fool.

'Myraa's World is named after the chief advocate of the religious cult now practiced by the surviving Herculeans who live on the planet. The cult allegedly strives to achieve what is called personality fusion, which is considered to be on the way to the omega point of mental development, and the practical end of integrated science. At this point the theorising becomes inarticulate, with talk of a hyperpersonal society and an emergence into a new reality. Needless to say, these claims are considered dubious by most students of the Herculean Empire. The cult is open only to Herculeans, and there are at best only five hundred individuals on Myraa's World, if not fewer. Many think of the planet as a kind of natural preserve. It is too far out in the galactic rim to be of much interest, and galactic cartographers consider it to be one of a chain of widely spaced *bridge* stars which link the spiral arms of our galaxy with the Magellanic Clouds.

'There are stories that Gorgias sometimes visits the planet, but there has never been any evidence for this . . .'

The one place where he was sure they would never look for him. Only a fool would be that naïve to think that he would find him there. And for that reason he could always go there, without fear. The other place was Earth.

'The current hunters are led by Rafael Kurbi, a psychologist of some note who has published works on the Herculean problem. He considers most histories of the war distorted and inaccurate. He argues that the Herculean "madness" was only an apparent phenomena, a function of their high metabolic rate and societal structure; but to us who live life more slowly it seemed like madness. He points out that their behavior after the start of hostilities cannot be taken as typical. Earthmen have a past which is filled with as much madness as the Herculeans'. He is fond of citing vast amounts of earth history, mostly pre-spaceflight and solar system bound, to support his views which have gained some influence in recent years.'

As he listened, Gorgias found himself almost siding with Kubri.

'. . . but the majority of Kubri's peers do not take his views seriously.

'Against this colorful background, Marko Ruggerio is writing his newest work, and we'll introduce him in a moment. The significant point about the composer's percussion cantata is that it is strongly influenced by the reconciliationist sentiments of men like Rafael Kurbi, who wish to make a final peace with Gorgias.

'And now let me introduce our viewers to Marko Ruggerio. Maestro Ruggerio, when do you expect to finish your new project?'

'A year, perhaps. I have hopes that Gorgias will come forward by then.'

Gorgias turned on the recorded video portion of the tape and looked at the two men sitting in the studio on Wolfe IV. Ruggerio looked like a weakling, with protruding front teeth and bushy eyebrows. The interviewer wore an idiot's grin, the perfectly acceptable grimace guaranteed not to upset anyone. He looked a bit tired from reading the material which had been prepared for him. They were fools, both of them; but one was an important fool who would make himself useful to him. Gorgias turned off the recording and wiped it clean from the ship's computer banks by pushing the clear button on his armrest panel.

The year was over. Tomorrow night Marko Ruggerio would very likely be at the top of his career. The city would be his, and exotic women from six worlds would try to see him personally after the concert, and everyone would go home greatly edified and full of pride in their Federation citizenship.

Who would see the true meaning of the event? No one, except Marko Ruggerio who might guess that he was dying by the hand of Gorgias the Herculean, for old time's sake.

For all the ancient wounds, this would be a small recompense.

A year ago he had bought a ticket for the concert on Wolfe IV, disguised as a merchant seaman who had emigrated to Wolfe from Sirius. Actually he shared an ancestry with that type, going back to ancient Asia on earth.

One had to be early for these events, very early.

He turned on the screen and cast some light into the dark ocean around him. There were some fish nearby and they fled from the light. The bottom was covered with silt and he saw a crab walk behind a rock.

Gorgias waited.

2. Percussion Cantata

'. . . hence this tremendous struggle to singularise ourselves, to survive in some way in the memory of others . . . this struggle, a thousand times more terrible than the struggle for life . . .'

– Unamuno

'What can I do to save them!' Danko thundered. Suddenly he tore open his breast and took out his heart and held it high over his head.

– Gorky

The great auditorium was filled to capacity. The lights were dim, and only a few stars were visible through the clear plastic dome. In a few moments they too would be obscured by the dark clouds which drove across the sky. A quarter of a million intelligent beings from six worlds filled the huge bowl with conversation, in at least ten different languages; and millions more watched at home, on a dozen different worlds, on every world tied into the subspace relay communications network.

The large circular platform in the center of the great bowl was black, waiting for the lights which would soon illuminate it. The lights themselves were glowing jewels set in a huge circle just below the clear dome; their glow was soft, waiting to burst into prominence, to shout their lights to the black area below.

Gorgias sat in the end seat of the last row, near the east

exit. He looked at the dark screen of the small monitor set at the end of his right armrest, where he would see closeups of the soloists at appropriate moments during the performance. He was dressed in the one-piece, close fitting dark blue jump suit once worn by the soldiers of the empire; now all markings of rank were gone, and a thick black cape made it certain that no one would recognise the ancient uniform. As if anyone would recognise the uniform of an enemy defeated centuries ago, Gorgias thought. Besides, the great variety of attires worn by the members of the audience made it certain that his would go unrecognised.

In the early morning hours he had swum ashore with his boots and cape tied in a bundle on his back. The breakers had been heavy on the beach, and he had been knocked over a few times before getting to dry sand. He had gone to a cheap hotel in the dock area and spent the day in his room listening to the radio. The bellhop, a moron eager to please, had twice during the day come up to his room to offer him bootleg bio-brew and a pair of twin young ladies from Earth. Earth itself! It might have been interesting, but he had refused.

In the auditorium now Gorgias turned briefly in his seat to look at the pickup camera on the wall behind him. In one brief moment before he had taken his seat he had placed the tiny pulse projector below one of the rotating lenses. The automatic scan of the camera would aim the weapon for him, at which time he would leave; that would be toward the end of the program when all the cameras would be focused on Mark Ruggerio taking his bows. As he went out he would release the automatic control which he wore around his wrist in the form of a watch. He would be gone when the weapon fired. Chances were that the composer would collapse on the spot; or, if he were hit in an arm or leg, he would die an hour later. The assassination weapon would self-destruct almost immediately after fulfilling its function. A swift death would be dramatic, Gorgias thought, a later one would be mysterious.

He regretted that he would not be around to see it happen; but after all, he had come to hear the concert. More could not be expected of him.

He thought, how strange to sit among so many people. He was an intruder attending a strange ritual; and he was certain that his unease was visible, tangible to all the beings around him. He was glad that the lights were dim. He looked up through the clear plastic dome and caught sight of a star just as a cloud obscured it. Another revealed itself almost instantly; it seemed friendly in its remoteness. The sight of stars and void had been the only home he had known for most of his three centuries of life. Yet surely the beings around him were not so different from him? For a moment he imagined himself a citizen of New Bosporus, with a position, friends, a female to love, regular decisions to make. He wondered what his mother had been like –

He stopped in mid-thought. A dark-haired female was looking up at him from two rows down. She sat turned in her seat, watching him. There was a faint smile on her lips. Abruptly she turned her back on him.

He wondered, do I stand out that much? She did not turn around again; he became sure that it had been just a casual stare. Suddenly he realised how unused to people he was, if he could not tell when people had just looked at him casually or were spying on him. It was a normal thing, after all, that intelligent beings looked at each other fairly regularly.

He looked at his watch. In one and one-half standard hours the light in the outer lock of his submerged ship would go on, to aid him when he swam to it from the beach. The underground shuttle which ran to the beach station came once every two minutes just outside the auditorium. He tried to imagine what could go wrong. *Use your imagination*, his father had told him long ago. *No matter how wild the thought, how insane it might seem, examine it. The sudden flash of insight, even the half formed suspicion may someday save your life. And never underestimate the ordinary and mundane, the simple – it might work better than something elaborate. Be elaborate, then be simple; don't be either for long.*

The buzz of conversation suddenly died down. The performance was about to begin. The lights dimmed into darkness, leaving only the intermittent starshine coming in through the clear canopy. The dark platform was suddenly full of light, coming from the circle of previously dim lights now reaching down to the platform with their intense beams. The audience sat in darkness. Gorgias felt secure in the gloom. He relaxed, feeling an almost pleasurable expectation at the events about to take place before him.

There were a hundred performers seated at the various instruments on the raised platform. Each set at an electronic console which was covered with oversize pushbuttons and giant levers. The only really novel presence on the stage was the massive percussion batteries – traditional instruments, with some of the designs dating back two and three thousand years to old Earth and the first solar confederation. There were drums of all shapes and sizes; two of the drums were taller than the male performers who stood ready to operate two mounted hammers hanging above each drum. Elsewhere on the stage stood celesta, xylophones, six grand pianos, giant triangles, massive bells, clickers, and iron anvils, and two gargantuan wooden blocks which would be struck by giant wooden mallets swinging freely on chains. All the instruments were wired for sound in the modern manner.

The male performers were in the majority, and were dressed in solid black one-piece dress suits; the female performers wore solid white one-piece suits, and most of them sat at the consoles.

Slowly the large stage was bathed in varying colored lights; one by one the beams splashed color on to the area, until the transformations ended in a deep blue which hung like a haze over the performers. Gorgias felt excitement in himself and mounting expectation in the audience around him.

There was a long silence, like the stillness before creation; or the lull before a storm.

A drum roll: coming up quietly from nowhere, growing louder, threatening to breath through the invisible barrier of silence, holding back. . . .

Unexpectedly the podium was covered with white light, and on it stood Marko Ruggerio and a female voice soloist. She began a weary song in high soprano, child-like in its purity, powerful in its completeness; there was not trace of strain in the face Gorgias saw in closeup on the small monitor.

The drums threatened menacingly.

In the moment before he understood, Gorgias felt anger at the intrusion. The audience reaction had been carefully calculated by the composer. From the very first it would be confronted with beauty and ugliness, war and peace, good and evil. It was all there, even in the black-white attire of the performers. He liked this even less than the tape of the interview with Ruggerio and its loaded historical sketch.

He was determined not to be swayed by the earthman's propaganda.

And yet the weary song echoed deeply in him, casting a strange glow around his consciousness; briefly he surrendered to its ache and charm. He dreamed of Myraa, the loveliness of her world; he longed to be with her, caress her. He tried to visualise her long hair and back as she stood by a window, facing the sunrise.

The song ended, the drums were triumphant. A giant mallet struck a wooden block with a deathlike thud.

The spell was shattered.

Then chaos reigned. The anvils chattered like the gnashing of metallic teeth. The giant drums thundered. A solid sheet of sound attacked Gorgias' ears: the clatter of old bones, skull against skull, the splintering sound of backs breaking like the boughs of strong trees; but there were no cries of the living here, only the abstract symbolic scheme of notes, the acceptable predigested reliving of the past.

The din grew quieter, spending itself like an angry ocean against an invulnerable sea wall with a clash of cymbals; a heroic melody came up from below and asserted itself tentatively. It was a well-constructed melody, well-formed, steadfast; it continued until it reached deafening proportions.

And stopped suddenly.

An inversion of the same melody appeared quietly, until it too grew monstrous and died.

Two heroic themes, mirror images of each other, one for each side of the great war.

Gorgias smiled inwardly, contemptuous of the composer's attempt at reconciliation. Who was he trying to convince? Certainly he was the only Herculean in the audience, and no one was aware of that. It seemed incredible that an earthman could mean this sort of thing seriously, and expect it to be honestly received. He could do without the mock generosity of the victor.

Now the first theme became distorted and ugly; and also its mirror image. Gorgias strained after the elements of order in the sequences as one by one they began to drop out.

Again the composer's spell caught him, and he followed the music as the eye of the beholder follows the lines of a painting to the area of central attention, there to be rewarded or disappointed.

He closed his eyes and thought of all the thousands upon thousands of Herculeans who had been murdered as prisoners toward the end of the war; he thought of those who had died in vaporiser chambers because earthmen had thought of them as freaks, biological mistakes; he thought of the giant lasers as they scorched the earth of whole planets, leaving only black carbon. And he remembered the vow which he had made in front of his father so long ago; the vow which he renewed each time he thought of it.

In the end only the lonely snake drums were left.

A bleak composition, by an obvious composer, who would not be remembered very long if he were fated to die a natural death; a composer of poster music whose fame would not be assured through his death at the hands of a Herculean.

His death would be a humiliating insult.

The last drum was silent.

Quickly, before the lights went up to bright, Gorgias got up from his seat, went up the double step into the aisle and walked to the exit. As he went out the door he pressed the automatic release on his watch which would activate the deadly toy he had left attached to one of the visual pickups.

The short tunnel led directly to the shuttle platform where an empty car was waiting to take him the one stop to the ocean front. It would all be over when he stepped off the shuttle at the other end.

Behind him in the great hall the house lights came to full brightness. Marko Ruggerio turned on the podium and bowed while holding the delicate hand of his soloist. The applause was enthusiastic. Softly the video cameras whirred, scanning the platform with their unconscious gaze.

And focused on his figure.

The applause grew louder.

The pulse weapon spat its deadly energy.

The applause faltered as the figure crumpled to the floor, still holding the hand of his soloist. She bent over him like a ministering angel.

The audience screamed. The sound hit the audio pick-ups, and in a moment had traveled three times around the planet: a seizure of a world's nervous system. Automatic devices adjusted the gain automatically, oblivious to the significance of the event. On the platform performers gathered around the stricken maestro, clustered like ants around a drop of honey.

* * *

The shuttle doors closed behind Gorgias only a moment before the audience reaction. In one minute the shuttle pulled into the ocean front station. Gorgias rushed out when the doors opened. The station smelled of brine and sewage. He rushed up a flight of stairs to the surface.

The sky was completely overcast now, and a strong wind was coming in from the sea. Gorgias climbed over the old wooden fence and dropped to the sand on the other side. He ran into the darkness toward the sound of strong breakers pounding the sand. Spray hit his face, and the smell of ocean was strong in his nostrils. He turned for a moment to look back. The dock area was dark; the only light came from the entrance to the underground shuttle. Five miles away, rising like a behemoth over lesser structures, the dome of the giant auditorium cast its light heavenward, only to have it hit the low hanging clouds rushing in from the sea to cover the land.

He took off his boots and his cape and tied them in a bundle with his belt. Then he walked boldly into the heavy breakers and threw himself into the water. After a few moments of battle he broke through the crests and swam forward, counting his strokes. The cape and boots were waterlogged and heavy around his neck. It would make them easier to handle when he submerged. In the dark clothing he knew he was invisible to anyone who might be watching from the shore.

A hundred yards out he dived for the ship. He opened his eyes in the water and saw the light, far below, at a depth of 200 feet. The airlock opened for him when he touched the button on the door. He swam inside, holding his breath. In one minute it had recycled and he drew in air. He untied the bundle from around his neck and held it. When the inner door opened he went immediately to the control area up front. He turned on the communications bands and swept through the range with the dial.

The entire planet was in an uproar. One commentator was saying something about the tragic interruption of a whole line of musical development as Gorgias tuned him out; another was accusing some political faction of the murder. Gorgias felt elated and alive as he ran back and forth across the bands.

He sat down at the command station and shut down most of his unessential instruments. Then he very carefully turned the ship around and moved forward into deeper waters, into depths which would be hard to match; into a darkness where he could wait safely, protected by the indestructible hull of his ship; safe against all weapons except those of the ancient masters who had built the ship and the very latest planet-based batteries of the Earth Federation.

High above the planet, above the ocean of water and air which protected him, he knew the hunters waited. They were the only threat he would have to consider seriously. And they would know his handiwork.

3. The Hunter

'You are myself, myself only with a different face . . .'

– Ivan Karamazov

The planet screamed.

On the large screen in front of him Rafael Kurbi watched what was going on in the large auditorium on Wolfe IV. A huge mob pressed in around the stage platform where the composer had fallen. It parted reluctantly to let the stretcher bearers reach the victim. The screams grew louder as Marko Ruggerio's body was carried out, leaving the crowd to mill around aimlessly.

He felt nothing for the popular composer. His death had been futile, but it would in time become better known than the man's music. Kurbi wondered what Gorgias would think if he knew what he felt? The act had Gorgias' mark all over it, there was little doubt about it in Kurbi's mind; but he knew the occasion of proof might never arise.

On the surface they were looking for an assassin's weapon which wasn't where it should be, and would probably self-destruct when they found it. Known firebrands were being arrested, and suspects were being picked up in the auditorium.

Kurbi leaned forward in his seat and spoke into the screen pickup. 'All officers – I suspect that Gorgias might try to leave the surface soon. Watch the night side near the terminator. Captain Scott, tell the authorities at New Bosporus what we suspect, so they don't go off and charge some innocent wretch with the slaying. Ruggerio is dead, isn't he?'

'Very much so,' Scott replied on audio.

'He must have planned this very carefully,' Kurbi said, 'and quite a while ago.' He thought of all the clues, the half-facts which had made it possible for him to witness Gorgias' newest action. How much of the trail had Gorgias set up for them all to follow? It was necessary that someone understand the Herculian's vengeance.

'He rarely improvises,' Scott said and broke the audio connection to carry out his orders.

Kurbi leaned back in his station seat and tried to relax. He wondered if Gorgias would try to leave Wolfe IV so soon after the assassination. It would be an obvious move, but it was impossible to depend on what would be obvious for him or not.

The trail was twenty years old for Kurbi, and he had learned early never to count on anything in connection with Gorgias. Dozens of hunters before him had given up in frustration and personal shame. Others had simply accepted it as their life's work, and had retired uncaring.

He was almost certain of one thing. He was not going to catch Gorgias on Wolfe IV. It was a basic assumption way down deep which seemed to him to be overwhelming in its correctness. Gorgias was going to come up with something simple. Later they would all understand what had happened..

Kurbi was tired. Twenty years of medical studies on Centauri, ten of service on a dozen worlds; and finally the command of a hunt which had taken so many lifetimes already, since the end of the great war over four centuries ago. An institutionalised stalking of a virtually impotent enemy who could never be more than a criminal nuisance, but who could still strike terror into the hearts of a huge starflung federation a thousand worlds strong, fearful of an old enemy who lived and thrived on that fear. Kurbi smiled ironically to himself.

He reached over to his panel and dimmed the lights in the control room, leaving only the glow of Wolfe IV on the screen. He closed his eyes, and the darkness conjured up the past in his brain. It was always able to assert itself easily whenever he tried to sleep or rest, and he had given up long ago trying to banish it. It was an old friend who had become irritating, very much like his superior, Julian Poincaré.

Ten years ago in a series of debates on earth he had finally convinced them to let him offer terms to Gorgias. He had finally gotten them to see that the past was not without fault, and that perhaps the Herculean could be persuaded to give up with honor.

He remembered his own high hopes that the matter would be settled at last.

Each group had had its own reasons for supporting him. Historians, eager to question an historical figure directly related to the great war, drawn by visions of possible caches of Herculean artifacts, technology and written records which Gorgias might know about, had given eager support to Kurbi in his softer attitude toward the old enemy.

Marko Ruggerio had sought him out then, to tell him of his planned work which he would unveil when Gorgias was captured, as an 'artistic act of reconciliation'. Kurbi had disliked the second rate composer even then for the trend hound he was. Ruggerio had waited and waited, and when Gorgias' surrender was obviously not forthcoming, he had announced the performance of his new work. Kurbi had come to Wolfe IV hoping that Gorgias would be drawn by the buffoon's music.

Kurbi remembered the words of Caddash, the old historian who came from a long line of historians, as he stood before the fossil which was the postwar dispositions commission – recalled to service on an ad hoc basis. *'We are not dealing with a real force,'* he had said, *'but with a weak individual, last of his kind and certainly not the equal of his forebears. This is not a new thing.'*

The most effective argument had come from the military, a self-serving thing on its own merit, but convincing to the listeners. Gorgias' Whisper Ship: the last of its type, a mysterious object worth much more than the life of the Herculean. If a settlement could be made with him, then it would be possible to find the location of the suspected base which was certainly filled with examples of pre-war Herculian technology, a prize which could not be ignored.

In the end he had been told to negotiate if possible; but he should not hesitate to destroy Gorgias if it became necessary. They had covered themselves perfectly.

Once their arrogance had made him angry. Now it was simply annoying. He would do what he believed in, regardless of any simple solutions which might offer themselves. Whatever the final outcome, no one on Earth would be able to undo it. He would present them with an accomplished fact, and by that time he would not care what they might say.

On the planet below, he could just barely make out the city of New Bosporus on the continental coastline, a sparkling light about to be covered by clouds. In the ocean to the west, a hurricane was beginning to wind its pinwheel faster and faster, and would soon threaten the land line with its fury.

A hunter gets to know his quarry.

Kurbi wondered if Gorgias would turn out to be as he imagined him. He wanted to meet with him face to face, alone, and talk, nothing more. He was sure he could open a dormant sector of the Herculean's character, an aspect clouded by a past which had washed him up on to the strange shore of the present; a past whose honors and practical loyalties were dead; a past which would shatter and fall away like an ancient mask of clay.

Kurbi often disbelieved in free will. If it existed it was very rare, the possession of the very powerful and unharried. The universe was made of a plentitude of facts; there was no justice, only facts. Justice had to be made, in the same way a man strikes a flame. At once it dies and must be made anew. The materials for fire and justice exist as facts, but the specific thing for a certain end must always be made. It can never sustain itself for longer than the life of its fuel, or the life of the man who brings it into existence.

Was Gorgias free? Certainly his life was taken up with the exercise of his own power and will – but to a trivial end, unworthy of his abilities. A rogue could often be a creative force in any culture, even if he could help topple a decaying civilisation. But there were many other things which Gorgias could do besides destroy himself.

He admired Gorgias. The Herculean bore an ancient name, with roots deep in Earth history, and very likely did not know what it had once meant.

Captain Scott's face appeared in the left-hand corner of the screen. 'Nothing so far,' he said.

'Keep the watch,' Kurbi answered. The other's picture faded. Scott was a good man, but he never said more about anything than was absolutely necessary.

Kurbi looked at the planet, a green and blue globe laced with clouds, wondering why intelligent creatures could not simply turn their backs on the stars and live out their lives on these beautiful islands swimming in the darkness. Why could we not be like cats, soaking up the sun, content to watch the horizon rather than try to find out what lay beyond it?

He knew the answer, as did every man who had ever been honest with himself somewhere in the dead of night. We like to have our lives threatened, we long for urgency and danger. Death stares us in the face like some monstrous abyss, and we rush toward it with the hope that we will come out on the other side.

He almost felt that these concerns might pass away from him, and he thought the lines he loved from two forgotten poets, lines which he always tried to think together. *I came 'out of the ninth month midnight' and someday death will be 'a quiet step into a sweet, clean midnight.'*

He felt a comfort in the patience of the words. At eighty, he knew, the lines were just beginning to come into his face. His hair was still black. His appearance would not change significantly until he was well past one hundred. His father had died at one hundred and seventy-five, almost reaching the full life span of those who were born on earth.

Many of the outworlders resented the lifespan of the earthborn, sneering at it as something artificial and sterile. A thousand jokes were told on the colonial worlds about the virility of earthmen, their strange medical practices and long-term outlooks. And yet they had come eagerly to acquire Earth's medical services whenever he had offered them. One day all of Earth's colonies would come into possession of the skills and luxuries which Earth had developed in its womb and was slowly sending out after her children.

One thing was certain: Gorgias had been wrong. Few would weep over the death of Marko Ruggerio on the colonial worlds; even fewer would be outraged. Flatterers and petty officials would tremble for a short time on Wolfe IV, and then the matter would be forgotten. Only Rafael Kurbi and a small group on Earth would continue thinking about Gorgias.

4. The Fiery Cloak

The whisper ship sprang from the dark ocean like a great fish urgently seeking a new medium. The ocean was rough as the outer winds of the hurricane prepared the waters for their assault on the land. Gorgias turned the ship toward the center of the storm. In a moment he was in the region of the highest winds, but the whisper ship was steady in the iron grip of its drive fields. At a thousand feet and just short of the storm's eye, Gorgias switched into whisper drive.

The ship's sudden disappearance created a vortex which swirled the ocean below into a huge whirlpool, raised the central windspeed of the hurricane, and effectively masked Gorgias' escape.

Gorgias peered into the scanner screen in front of him. The gray-white glow coming from it lighted his face in the dark cabin. He was running the ship on minimum power to help hide his escape. He had left normal space while still coordinate with Wolfe IV; the hunters would be looking for a ship which would first move away from the planet and then slip into hyperspace. It was the first time he had tried this maneuver, and it had worked. There was no sign of pursuit on the screen. The storm had covered his tracks well.

One-half standard hour later there was still no sign of

the hunters. Eventually he was sure someone would notice that the storm was not following its normal path; they would find enough energy scatter from his change over into drive to extrapolate his probable vector away from the planet. But he would see to it that his trail would lead to a dead end. He would make sure that they could not effectively follow him now.

The trick was fairly simple, but few had ever had the courage to try it. He turned his drive up to its highest index; then he set the ship for an automatic whisper course toward Antares – directly at the giant red star; more correctly, where Antares would be in normal space. His ship would pass directly through the star. They would be able to determine what he had done, but it would be impossible to fix his direction after he came out on the other side. He had learned this ploy as a child. There was some danger to it. He would, after all, be playing with a star's magnetic and gravitational fields which continue to exist as forces in hyperspace.

To the hunters his trail would end in the heart of the great red furnace; to confuse them still further he would re-enter normal space before going through the star. Perhaps they would be led to suspect that he was hiding on one of Antares' dark bodies, one of the six massive dark companions which were the red star's planets.

He sat back and relaxed; he would lose them now.

The time had come is disappear, to rest, and to think of the future. He would go to his father's base and visit his tomb. He still thought of it as his father's base, even after three centuries. It had been another universe then, another person who had performed the burial. Had it been another person who had made the vow of vengeance? That part of him was still the same and would survive as long as he continued to exist. He felt it as an indestructible bundle of energy, wound tight inside his chest. The day would come when its full fury would be unleashed, and all the ancient enemies would flee before him.

At the base he would add more crystalline memory units to the ship's computers; he would continue his study of the arsenal; and he would continue his search for the one weapon which could put him in a superior position over the earthborn. There were many weapons in the arsenal which he had not yet mastered; someday he would be called upon to teach others their use. He would have to be ready.

At the war's end a small army of Herculeans had fled into smaller Magellanic Cloud. Someday he would find them; then would begin his offensive war against the earthborn.

* * *

Ten standard hours went by. His approach to Antares was represented by means of a three-dimensional geometric pattern projected on the gray field of the screen. Animated lines of differing colors clearly showed the gravitational and spatial disturbances which accompanied the normal space-time existence of the large star. Gorgias slipped into normal space and looked at the awesome red giant, then the screen became gray again as he returned to non-space.

On the gray screen the colored lines danced in a frantic effort to mirror the reality of the forces surrounding the star. In one moment the geometric representation was a series of circles, in the next cubes within cubes with superimposed triangles. The model was adequate to represent the quantitative aspects of the forces emanating from the star. it would never capture the reality.

Before he had time to fully consider the risk, Gorgias' ship was passing into the star; the geometric model struggled to represent what was happening. Gorgias gripped the armrests of his station and tested. What unknown forces could tear him and his ship apart at any moment? Here he was passing through the power points of all reality, yet he felt sure that he risked nothing.

He was in the heart of Antares. The screen diagram

was pulsating furiously. Gorgias watched his progress with no emotion, ready to correct his course at the slightest sign of instability in his transit of the star's field in non-space.

Briefly all the lines in the diagram turned red. The warning light went on in front of him; and died just as quickly. The lines in the diagram grew more stable, lost their red color; he knew he was on the other side.

Slowly he relaxed his grip on the armrests and let out a sigh. He could do it again if he had to. Swiftly he leaned forward and punched a course for the open cluster in Hercules, on a course for his father's base. His base, he reminded himself.

He got up from the controls and went aft to his sleeping quarters, a small cubicle which contained a large bunk equipped with zero-g controls, a bathroom and a small mess. He ate an instant meal and went to bed, setting the controls for zero-o.

For a time his sleep was unbroken, but later troublesome dreams appeared like dark clouds on an infinitely clear horizon. He seemed poised above a great abyss; a great weight pressed on his back. At any moment he expected to be crushed by it, or be pushed into the space below; but nothing happened.

He was frozen into his dream, unable to wake up.

After an age, he was looking across the plane of the galaxy, over a plain of stars to the glowing incandescent hub. There were huge fireflies clustered around it, the open globular clusters in their orbits, jeweled groupings of stars; and one of them was his home.

Thoughts crossed the void. He reached out. The embodiment was not complete.

He opened Myraa's eyes from within suddenly, glowing inside her. He sensed the presence of space around himself, distinct from the inverted spaces of subjective time.

Then she hurled him back from her eyes, back into an endless falling toward a floor of icy fire.

He tried to see the sun and ocean shore. Her thoughts

crossed the void after him, first making him remember, then making him forget; making him sleep for another age....

The pressing dream-fear dissolved itself, and he slept.

5. Cry Into the Echo

In an orbit twenty-five thousand miles above Wolfe IV, Rafael Kurbi sat in front of his screen talking to his superior, Julian Poincaré, Earth's highest ranking intelligence officer, via subspace relay channels. He was a stocky man with a low voice and an unsettling sense of humor which he used to frighten underlings who didn't know better. He was thirty years Kurbi's senior.

'Well, did he or did he not get away from you?'

Kurbi said, 'He seems to have left the planet. A certain ocean area to the west of New Bosporus shows traces of what might have been a ship slipping into low drive.'

'In the atmosphere? Could his ship take that kind of handling?'

'I wouldn't be surprised. I suspect that he might have aggravated a storm in that area, using it for cover.'

'By now,' Poincaré said, 'he's set a clever false trail for you to follow. You've probably disappointed him by not following it.'

'I keep wondering – maybe he hasn't left the planet at all.'

For a moment Poincaré's screen image wavered, as if his impatience had suddenly disturbed the subspace link with earth. The intelligence chief shook his head. 'It looks bad for you, Kurbi. To date you've had little or no result. What do you think?'

'Gorgias will turn up eventually,' Kurbi said. 'This was a long shot. I wasn't expecting much.'

'Where?'

'Myraa's World. I don't know when, but I'm sure of it.'

'You're sure of it – but in the meantime he'll set himself up from another stunt. I know we can't prove he killed Ruggerio, but you and I are sure, aren't we?'

'See there, you *do* believe me, don't you?'

'I do, sure, but I have trouble communicating my faith to the big thumbs around me.'

'They can go put their heads into a nova,' Kurbi said.

'Stop that! Don't parody me, Raf.'

'Gorgias has put a lot of space between his tricks in the past,' Kurbi said seriously.

'And you told me that all hatred dies in time.'

'It does, in time.'

'Nit picker.'

'You'd rather see him dead?'

'I don't care much for myself,' Poincaré said, 'but everyone seems to know better.'

Kurbi tried to grasp what was going on inside Gorgias' mind. If he could only meet him, for only a moment, convince him to help retrieve something of the civilisation which had made him. If Gorgias died, with him would perish a key to the past, a past essential to a proper understanding of Earth's history; with him would die all the difference in culture which any civilisation must periodically absorb in order to survive. Four centuries ago the Earth Federation had destroyed an enemy completely, absorbing little if anything from him, and turning its back on the few proud survivors. The loss had been irreparable, its effect on subsequent centuries deadening.

He was sure there was more to Herculean culture than the war had revealed. There must have been philosophers, scientists, musicians and poets – much more than even

Gorgias knew. He was much too young. And it had all perished.

The sense of urgency quickened again in Kurbi's mind. He had to find him, talk to him, make him understand that there were other things in life for him. On earth bio-engineers could clone his genetic materials and revive a portion of his stock. In time his descendants would intermarry with federation citizens and the few survivors on Myraa's World. If Gorgias was as long-lived as suspected, he would have chance to see his sons grow up and come into their full mental powers, channeling them into achievement, not hatred. Surely the prospect of banishing the past could be an attraction for him.

He thought of the surviving Herculeans, leading quiet, hermit lives, withdrawn from creation. Gorgias was vigorous and intelligent, the kind of leader they needed to pull them out of their stoicism, a shocked posture which had grown directly from the defeat of their empire.

' . . . maybe you need a rest,' Poincaré was saying. 'When was the last time I saw you bodily?'

'I don't think so, I've got to see this through to the end.'

'Whose end, yours or his?'

'Neither. I'm going to Myraa's World, as soon as I can get ready.'

Poincaré threw up his hands. 'I won't stand in your way, up to a point. But say you lose a ship or lives, or something . . . someone will have me for breakfast.'

'They'd spit you out,' Kurbi said smiling, 'you'd taste too bitter, Julian.'

Poincaré snorted and broke the connection. Somewhere, Kurbi knew, sub-space communications engineers on remote relay stations light-years away were wondering what rude fellow made a practice of breaking expensive connections so abruptly.

Kurbi looked at his reflection in the gray surface of the screen, feeling its thoughts from the inside. It stared back at him as he watched it for some sign of madness or obsession. He dreamed of all the things he had not had time for yet. All the good music, better than anything Ruggerio had ever done; all the women he could still have; all the luxuries of the pleasure palaces on earth where he might rest in stately repose while his mind scaled the peaks of an infinite dream reality which could never exist.

He might have another son, one who could be a credit to him. He thought of Grazia, dead these forty years; frail, transparent Grazia with her long black hair and large sad eyes, dying of a strange sickness like an exotic flower wrenched suddenly from the garden which was Earth. He remembered her swimming gently in a tropical pool, and the way he had watched her come out of the water naked and lie down on the green grass; he remembered a distant fear which had crossed his mind then. He had remembered it when she had been taken from him, and he remembered it now, and it seemed to him as if the future had cast its shadow into a happier past in order to torment him. Looking back from any instant after her death, the chain of events seemed to be inevitable, bound in iron.

He had wandered after Grazia's death, looking for something useful to do on a party planet filled with mad revels and speeding around the sun in a perfectly adjusted orbit, a world where the only imperative was that its power not be disturbed. He came to understand why the outworlders distrusted visitors from the home planet. They paid for Earth's protection while hating a life style which could not possibly serve them.

Power on Earth was localised in strong individuals who did very little with it themselves except attend to its preservation, and dispense it upon the petition of those who needed it. Anything was permitted as long as it did not constitute a basic change in anything. The continued hunting of Gorgias was a form of insurance which no one dared to cancel.

Some of those who could see beyond their own noses without personal fear were on the postwar adjustments commission. Poincaré was one such, had been one such when he had met him. For a short time they had both seen more in Gorgias than the flickering fear which had drawn the appointed hunters over the last three hundred years. They had shared a dream of a different future.

As the decades had gone by, Poincaré seemed to understand, even while his own life had grown more trivialised and he had become more fearful of his own position. Kurbi had finally developed the impression that Poincaré had determined that less and less should happen each day to disturb his life; and slowly the potential meaning of the search for Gorgias had become a complex of practicalities between them.

Kurbi had grown to develop a kinship for the Herculean, feeling that if anyone could ever understand what was at stake, it would be Gorgias. He admired his self-reliance, his power to move by his own counsel. Gorgias' hatred was a natural force, moving by a seemingly sudden inspiration. His instincts were surer than his intellect; but then instinct was nature's intellect, honed to automatic perfection by millions of years of trial and error, freeing the organism to do other things besides pay attention to essentials.

Gorgias had made few mistakes, but in time the situation might become too complex for him to handle without the most meticulous planning; then he would overreach himself and act in partial ignorance. Kurbi knew that if Poincaré were to question him on this, he would have to plead for time, justifying his own instincts with the analogies a hunter draws between himself and his quarry.

He would have to try to complicate things for Gorgias as much as possible by waiting for him in force near Myraa's World. This time he was certain Gorgias would go there. The Herculean would expect him to follow a blind trail from Wolfe IV. For once he would not do the logical thing.

He could not abandon the hunt. It would have to end

his way, or with Gorgias' death. That final alternative filled him with dread and anguish, and a weary sorrow; yet he knew he would not shrink from it.

On earth they would hail him for the act, but he would have to live with his failure for the rest of his days.

6. Impromptu

The forest below the whisper ship was a mass of broken green mirrors reflecting the sunlight of Izar II. The original Izar was only 173 light-years from Earth, but the second colony was ten thousand light-years toward the galactic center. Its link to the solar system's federation was a hyperspace beacon – a lighthouse radiating into non-space, guiding the three or four yearly ships to the fledgling settlement.

Gorgias had noticed the prominence of the beacon while still in whisper drive, a splash of red sweeping in a wide arc on his screen – and three concentrated beams penetrating deeply into warp-space toward the galactic perimeter.

It was an easy stop on the way to his father's base, although he had never approached it from this angle. He had decided to stop and take a look, wondering if there might be something for him on the planet. Perhaps he could take a captive, or perform a small act to annoy the colonists from Earth before continuing. No one would expect him to appear on the planet circling Izar II, especially if he had not planned it himself.

He knew in the back of his mind that he was reluctant to see his father's base again. There was something about the empty installation which half frightened him. He remembered the crowded auditorium on Wolfe IV, comparing it with the deserted levels of the old base deep inside an airless rock circling an unknown star in the galaxy's center. The planet below him was inhabited by people who were his enemy, he told himself, reason enough to delay him.

He felt the burden of isolation disappear inside him as he brought the ship down near the edge of a large clearing. He sat back at his command station and dreamed of people coming across the grassy clearing on the screen, people who would welcome him as soon as he stepped out of the ship. He reached by his armrest and pushed the button to open the sidelock. There would be no one for him outside. He felt the long time silence in his throat, knowing that he would have to go to Myraa's World to speak with his own kind. He felt the warm air coming into the ship through the open lock and he got up to go out.

He came out through the sidelock and looked at the huge waxlike leaves which had produced the mirror effect from above. The air was warm, filled with the smell of growing things. The sunlight was a yellow wash on the greenery; a breeze moved the tree branches with a soft rustling sound.

There was no sign of people. A quick scan of the planet had revealed the main colony to be a hundred miles to the east of this clearing. He could see one of the beacon towers standing on the wooded mountain north of the clearing. He assumed that it was checked regularly by rangers from the colony, or from a small nearby settlement which he had missed.

The humanoid natives were few and far between. He had learned from his computer banks that most of them had died of a plague which had swept the planet fifty years ago. From the limited information in the ship's history banks he had not been able to find out whether earthmen had brought the plague with them, or if the disease had been in progress when they had arrived. In any case, the colonists had saved the remainder of the native population and had been permitted to settle. There were more than fifty thousand earthmen on the planet, and no one knew how many natives. He knew that if he wanted more information about Izar II he would have to land on a highly developed Federation planet and record from their transmitting libraries, or find a public information booth punch-index. It might be worthwhile someday to find out if the natives had any grudges against earthmen.

Gorgias took a deep breath and looked up at the yellow sun. Storm clouds were moving toward it from the south, threatening rain.

He began to walk across the clearing toward the forest, stretching his muscles, enjoying the feel of soft ground under his boots, looking at the irregularity of the earth around blades of grass, so new after the perfect interior geometry of the ship.

It began to rain by the time he reached the trees, and he ran in under the protection of the huge leaves. Here the very shadows had a green tint in them. Soon the moisture was running in huge rivulets from the trunks and branches, giving the forest a smell of wet bark and mint leaf. Some of the leaves caught the rain like huge goblets, and overflowing let loose their fill on to the path in front of him.

Drawn by the forest, he continued down the path, noticing that it was a well-used trail. He quickened his pace and came to a branch. One led up the mountain toward the tower, and the other probably continued around the mountain.

He took the upward path, wondering about the beacon tower. It was probably one of three or four, forming a square or triangle on the planet's surface, a huge figure linking the colony with the parent federation. Messages could be sent to nearby stars using the net, as well as guiding in ships.

After a half-hour Gorgias emerged on the mountain top. Above him stood the tower, five hundred feet of metal with a cage on top and a spidery stairwell leading up to it.

He turned around in the rain and looked down at the water-soaked forest. He brushed away some of the rain running down his face and pushed back the hair plastered to his forehead. His uniform was waterproof, so he felt mostly dry. Far away in the clearing below, the ship sat on the ground, its polished hull looking dull in the downpour. It was just barely visible over the trees from where he stood.

He turned around and noticed the little wooden hut hidden under the latticework of the tower. He walked between the huge legs of the tripod structure and through the open door of the hut.

There was an odor of rotting bark inside. The floor was made of dirt. He saw a table, a chair and an old cot in the dim light. There was one window by the door partially covered by a rag. The little hovel was probably used by maintenance people when visiting the tower. It didn't look as if anyone came here often.

Gorgias sat down in the wooden chair and breathed in the wet air. The chair groaned under him when he moved. What if he destroyed the tower, he thought. They could fix minor damage, but what if he blotted out the planet's presence on their simulation maps and navigational tanks? Or better still, what if he readjusted the beacon to lead ships into their sun?

It would be an easy thing to do. No one knew he was here, and only the patient few, if any, would ever suspect that he had been responsible.

A sound startled him and he sat up rigidly in the chair, making it creak loudly. Someone was coming up the path to the tower, he was sure of it. He sat perfectly still, listening to the gentle footsteps. He got up and went to the rag-covered window and peered outside through a hole in the cloth.

A figure wearing a green coverall was coming up the path slowly, grasping a tall walking stick in its hand, hunching over a bit under the pack on its back. A wide-brimmed hat shielded the face from view and the rain.

The figure stopped a dozen feet from the door. Gorgias moved gently away from the window, back toward the cot against the rear wall.

The figure came inside with its head lowered, its wide hat dripping water on to the dirt floor. The person was not very tall, Gorgias noticed, but thin enough to appear taller from a distance.

The girl dropped her pack on the ground behind her and leaned her walking stick against the wall near the door. Then she took off her hat with a sweeping motion which threw droplets of water at Gorgias. He caught her eye suddenly and she stared back, surprised, unblinking. She did not seem frightened.

For a few moments he could think of nothing to say. This was a colony of a direct colony from earth, so she would very likely address him in an earth-derived language. When she spoke, he would know how to answer her to prevent any immediate suspicion about his origin.

'Hello,' she said smiling, and continued looking directly at him.

He nodded to her uncertainly.

She said, 'My name is Idella. I assume yours is the small yacht in the clearing?' She waited for his answer, but continued immediately when he did not speak. 'Oh, we get well-to-do folk from the Earth sector of the galaxy out this way – once or twice a year at least. What's your name?'

He tried to smile at her instead of answering, thinking it would be better for her to draw her own conclusions.

'The rain caught you here and you took shelter – ' She paused, examining him carefully with her eyes. She had long brown hair which she wore in a bun. She came up close to him suddenly and he saw that her eyes were green. 'Can you understand me?' she asked.

Gorgias nodded. He was unused to standing in another's gaze, and the sense of presence he felt emanating from her was startling. He was perfectly alert in front of her, in a way he had not known for a long time. The auditorium on Wolfe IV had been impersonal, but in front of Idella he felt completely real. On Wolfe IV he had been an avenging ghost, cold and bloodless; but now he could almost sense her heartbeat in front of him.

'Good,' she said, 'we can talk as long as it rains.' She sat down in the chair with a thump and put her wet hat on the wooden table. 'For a minute there I thought I would have to use sign language with you – that would have been dreary, wouldn't it?'

As he continued looking at her, he was glad that she was talking so much, leaving him his secrecy. He could almost forget what he was here for as he looked at her unafraid expression.

'Later I'll have to go upstairs on the tower and check the beacon instruments,' she said, 'or people like yourself would not find us in a decade. Even a small error in warp-space becomes huge, and of course visual fixes are impossible. Even in normal space no one can see with all the galactic dust and stuff, not until they're almost on top of us – which can't be done without the beacon.' She paused and raised one eye at him questioningly. 'How's that – did I explain it good? Huh?'

He nodded. 'How old are you, Idella?'

She smiled. 'You've got a nice voice,' she said.

'Thank you,' he said imitating her centauri anglo-germanic sounds. He guessed that she might be twenty years old.

'I'm eighteen earth years old,' she said proudly. 'Hey, are you going to come into town with your yacht?'

'Town?'

'About two miles south,' she said.

'I don't think so – I saw the beacon as I went by. I didn't plan to stop. . . .'

'Are you alone? Aren't there others – maybe girls from Earth aboard?'

'No,' he said. 'Will you be here at the tower long, Idella?'

'Nope,' she said, bringing her knee up and resting her heel on the chair's edge, 'I've got to go home as soon as I check upstairs for father. Usually he sends my three brothers, but I'm more reliable, he says, in how I adjust the beacon if it's drifted any.'

They were both silent for a while.

'Goodbye, Idella,' he said. He went out into the rain quickly and was fifty feet away before she shouted after him.

'Hey, what's your name!'

He waved to her over his head without turning around, and quickened his pace back to the ship.

* * *

The rain stopped before he reached his ship. He knew what he would have to do as soon as Idella left the tower. The accident he had in mind would work only once. Then they would take the beacon instruments apart. Maybe Idella would be blamed for the misadjustment?

Suddenly he disliked the idea that she might be blamed. He could almost feel her outrage if she were to be accused. He knew that she would be sure of her adjustments of the beacon. No, he thought, the drift would be too large for anyone to blame her. They would know it had been deliberate.

He went into the ship through the open lock and moved forward into the small control room, where he sat down in the command station and pushed the button to close the lock.

He waited, occasionally turning the ship's telescopic screens to look at the tower to see if he could see Idella. Finally he caught a glimpse of her coming down the stairwell.

An hour later he decided that it was safe to go back. He went back into the ship's weapons storage where he took a small bomb off the rack. He let himself out through the lock and in a few minutes was halfway across the clearing. The grass was wet, cleaning his boots to shine through the clouds as he entered the forest and found the path.

He hurried up the hill, thinking of Idella and how far removed she was from what he was about to do.

There was no sign of her when he reached the hut. He went inside and dug up the soft dirt under the wooden table with his hands. He put the bomb into the hole and covered it up. He would be able to set it off at will from space, but hopefully he would not have to do that. The bomb was just a back-up if his other idea went wrong.

He came out of the hut and started up the spiral stair, reaching the top in a few minutes. He could see the ship clearly across the downward slope of trees. The hull glinted in the emerging sunlight. For a moment he thought of it as a yacht, as Idella did; but the image was not very convincing to one who knew its functional interior and had known it for more than twenty decades as a cramped extension of his own will. Yet he was sure that no matter what the interior, it would not have disappointed Idella. Again and again he found himself looking at things with her eyes.

He stepped through the small entrance into the beacon shelter. The instrument stood on an anchored tripod. There was a plastic hemisphere cover over it which he lifted back on its flexi-hinges. After a minute of study the adjustment settings became clear to him.

The entire mechanism was made to be taken apart easily, in case of emergencies. First he set the coordinates for Izar. Then he removed the setting face and adjusted the mechanism to read at Idella's last setting. Now the beacon would direct ships into the star, while continuing to read correctly on the dial. He snapped the face back on.

He stood up. It had been very easy, he thought, but then again what kind of security did this beacon need? It had never been in any kind of real danger, and not much could really ever go wrong in its straightforward design. Its own drift probably never exceeded one per cent, and it was kept adjusted below that so that ships could come out of warp close to the colonial world and not have to travel far in the Izar system to reach their destination, even though it would not be too much trouble to do so. Who would come out here just to do what he had done?

'Well, so you're still here,' Idella's voice said from behind him. He spun round to face her. 'Scared ya, huh?' She moved past him in the cramped shelter and picked up her hat from behind the beacon tripod. 'Forgot it after the rain stopped,' she said while putting it on. 'Came back to see the view?'

He watched her face as she noticed the open instrument cover.

'What were you doing looking at the controls?' she asked, looking at him sternly.

'That . . . stuff interests me,' he managed to say. 'I didn't touch anything.'

'You could see *through* the cover,' she said while closing it. He could tell that she was not too suspicious yet. He would have time to leave. For a moment he had been worried that he would have to restrain her, maybe even taken her as a hostage if she had been able to signal for help. He was almost afraid of the idea of taking her with him. He told himself that erotically she was too young and shallow to interest him. He would not be able to relate to her. Yet he almost cared what she thought about him. He sensed his own fear behind the thought. Her very existence embarrassed him.

'By the way, who are you – what's your name?'

He would have to make something up.

She turned away from him to look down into the trees below. 'Oh, lookit, here comes my father and brother – they're looking for me, I'm very late. You'll like them, and I found you all by myself!'

He tried to see where she was looking and saw no one. He would have to go quickly now.

He rushed for the stairwell and began to clamber down the metal spiral, his boots clattering on the narrow rungs. She was behind him shouting, 'Where are you going? You don't have to be afraid!' She still did not suspect anything. Around and around he went, leaving her behind and above him.

He reached the ground and ran down the path into the trees and down the hillside, and still she was behind him. She was on the slope behind him when he reached level woodland, and gaining. When he reached the clearing, her voice was an echo coming out of the trees after him. The sun became bright in his eyes suddenly, and he knew that he was afraid of her. If she caught up with him, he would have to knock her down, shattering her illusion about him. He was afraid to have her see him differently.

The hull of the ship was warm around the lock entrance as he staggered inside. He stopped and turned to look back. She was running through the clearing now, and on the mountainside behind her he glimpsed two other figures in the trees. One of them shouted, 'Idella, come back!'

He watched her draw closer, running through the grass like some swift four-footed creature, jumping over rocks at her feet, coming closer to him with every second.

He closed the lock and the inner lock.

He went forward to the command station, trying to ignore his thoughts, and lifted the ship from the clearing. In a few moments he was five miles above the planet, moving slowly west above snow-white clouds.

Should he destroy the beacon now, or hope that it would be left alone long enough to catch a starship in its trap? The entire situation was wrong. They would check the instruments carefully after questioning Idella. He could destroy all the towers with his shipboard weapons, or he could set off his planted bomb. The purpose was to cut off the colony world from the rest of the Federation for an annoying period of time.

He turned the ship in a huge circle in the upper atmosphere, bringing it back over the tower and clearing. He pressed the remote detonator button on his armrest and watched the tower flare up on the screen. The wet forest began to smoke around it and caught fire.

He made a sharp turn and came back even lower for another look. The explosion had made a huge crater on the mountain top.

He cut in the automatics and let the ship find the rest of the beacon system. He found the other two towers of the triangle only fifty miles apart. He made a run on each tower with his laser cannon, leaving two huge scars on the land.

Then he searched for Idella's small town and found it only a few miles from the first tower. It was a very small community compared to the actual colony a hundred miles east. There was one street with a dozen buildings. He brought the ship in slowly and set fire to the roofs of the houses with his laser. For Idella's sake, those inside would have enough time to escape.

In another minute he was over the clearing again, and he saw two men standing next to Idella in the grass, all three looking at the blazing hillside and the black smoke coming up from the town. He speeded up the ship for a swift pass which he knew would knock them to the ground with a whistling sound.

In a moment the clearing was far behind him, and the ship was climbing starward. A thousand miles out he turned on the whisper drive and the ship slipped into gray ashes. There was no beacon on the screen.

He felt nothing. Idella was an absurd image in his mind, laughing at him.

7. 'A Bitter Native Land . . .'

'Thy soul shall find itself alone . . .
Now are thoughts thou shalt not banish.'

The whisper ship flickered out of non-space with the ppp of a musical note which suddenly becomes a sustained sound, the dash-dash-dash of a broken line which at once becomes unbroken, continuous.

Around the ship the stars of the Hercules Globular Cluster were lanterns hanging in the night. Space was thick with interstellar dust glowing brightly, wrapping the myriad huddling suns in a shimmering field. They were hot stars, close together, varicolored and dazzlingly bright. The cluster of fifty thousand suns was one of the galaxy's ornaments, a striking object even in the lenses of faraway worlds.

The core of the cluster, thirty light-years in diameter, contained the greatest concentration of stars; from a distance the core was a solid mass of light, as if some cosmic craftsman were planning to create a super star from the gathered suns.

A hundred hours at full power it had taken to bring him here. He could live out a dozen lifetimes among these stars and not be found. Gorgias looked at the grand display on the screen. Something much like reverence came over him, as if here before him were the beginning of all things; each star was one of thousands of silent beings who ruled all the universe from this place. Here his past melted away, seemed small and uninteresting by comparison. . . .

He broke the spell with one effort and set the final coordinates for his destination.

The star which was his destination was a small, white-hot star near the center of the cluster, shrouded in a dust cloud one-half light-year long. Its one planet was a chunk of rock six thousand miles in diameter, airless, its sky dominated from horizon to horizon by the starless darkness of the dust cloud, and the pale, partially darkened light of its sun.

Gorgias brought his ship in carefully, moving slowly forward through the cloud which obscured the view on the screen. Here and there the cloud was suddenly shot through with light, the lances of the ruling gods. Slowly the ship continued to move forward, toward the area of the cloud which continued to gain in brightness. Gorgias looked watchfully at the coordinate readings on his control panel.

The screen grew noticeably brighter. Gorgias leaned forward toward the screen. Even as a child the coming view had never failed to move him.

The ship burst out of the dark cloud, into an area of light devoid of all but one star. There the dust cloud was nearly transparent, and the light was splintered by it into a thousand flashes and beams cutting through the gas. Home was here, the warm huddling place which had never been found by the earthborn; here his father rested in his tomb, and from here would come the ancient nemesis against the earthgiants.

Soon the barren, craggy surface of the planet took up half the viewscreen; and a little later the polar mountains sprawled below the ship. Gorgias put the ship on automatic for the final approach.

The tunnel entrance gaped at him on the screen like the barrel of some huge gun set in the side of the mountain, designed to fire at a tangent to the surface. Slowly the ship floated up near to the entrance and was swallowed up.

A little ways in the tunnel became tighter. The inside was polished smooth and with a minimum of power the ship slid forward to its berth far below. As it came through locks opened and shut to let it through.

The berth was a curved notch cut in a huge block of concrete. The ship fit it perfectly. It was the only one in the row of six places. Gorgias sat still for a few moments. Homecoming, if he could call it that, was always a time filled with mixed feelings. It would fill him with elation, a sense of safety; and also with a sense of entombment, the false finality of the locks opening and closing for him as he came into the base through the tunnel. He worried at times that the mechanism would fail, and the locks would never open again, and he would be trapped here forever.

He got up from the command station and went to the vertical airlock. He pushed the bypass buttons and went up the ladder to the top hatch. He opened it and climbed out on to the ship's hull. From there he stepped out to the concrete walk which surrounded the vessel on three sides.

His footsteps echoed as he went through the huge open door set in the rock cavern wall. He continued down a long, unlighted hallway until he came to another heavy metal door. Like the first one it too was partially open.

The lighting in the war room was bright, much brighter than out in the ship's berths. Gorgias sat down in one of the heavy chairs arranged around the polished metal table. The room still retained its antiseptic odor, a sign that the airconditioning system was still working.

Centuries had gone by and the polished table had not lost its mirrorlike luster. Once the faces of great leaders and strategists had been reflected in it, as they debated and planned and shouted at each other across its surface.

Home.

The base had never been conquered, but it could never defend itself in attack now. That would never happen, he told himself, but still *home* had to be thought of as a place beyond reach, beyond danger, where all hopes could be stored. He had never seen New Anatolia, not even three-dimensional representations of it. He had been born in space, and throughout his childhood his father had kept the visual records from him, fearing that the sight of them would destroy his spirit. Gorgias knew that there were tapes made during the war somewhere in the base; but up to now he had not searched for them.

Almost word for word he still remembered his father's account of the destruction of New Anatolia, the home world of the Herculean Empire. It was a beautiful world, the plaything of two stars which passed it among themselves in a shared orbit, a perfect figure eight which took two years to complete.

A hundred ships from earth, built for one purpose: to destroy New Anatolia, break the will of the empire. They came with their heavy mounted lasers and sun reflectors. The entire surface of the planet had been marked off for each ship. They came as if to mow the lawn and destroy pests.

They struck – all at once, each ship in its own special area. They left the planet a baking cinder, the ground carbonised to a depth of fifty feet, the oceans a mass of steam pushing its way over the black surface like a fog.

A billion souls. It had not been an overpopulated planet. The corpses did not have time to bleed. The firestorms had swept across the continents, searing the lungs of every creature, setting fire to bone and tissue like waste paper. The fine dust which remained could not possibly bleed.

Here and there a few had survived, only to be forced to the surface to breathe the fine dust and alien air; and shrivel up into dry sacks filled with brittle bones. Ornaments to dot the dark surface. . . .

As he sat in the chair, Gorgias felt the subliminal hum of the vast machine which kept up the base's air, heat and light. The generators drew their raw power from the thermal core of the planet by means of a giant alloy finger stuck deeply into the center of the world's core. The machines would continue to function and repair themselves indefinitely, as long as the planet continued to exist.

New Anatolia's gravity had been one and one-half g's. Here it barely reached one-g. Gorgias remembered that his father had never talked about the home world as it had been before its death. He had described its rape to him a thousand times, but it had been too much for him to describe its past beauties.

He looked at the glare of the lights in the surface of the table; he looked at his fingertips touching their twins in the mirrored finish. He wondered if this time he would find the weapon he had sought here so many times before. Myraa had told him about it shortly after his father's death. It was reportedly a small object – a six-inch long cylinder, a casing filled with a crystalline substance. Locked in its electrical matrix was the pattern for a fully armed division of Herculean troops.

He already had the control tripod. All he would have to do was find the cylinder and plug it into the tripod panel, and all the power of his ship would go into the instant creation of fifteen thousand fighting men.

The thought filled him with a sense of power. He saw the troops appearing out of nowhere, to sweep the field of battle of all the earthborn. He had to find the cylinder. From that day onward he would not have to strike and hide; he would be able to challenge the enemy openly.

Yet in all the years that he had come here, he had never found the cylinder. It had never come into use during the war; Myraa had assured him that no earth-giant knew of its existence. Perhaps it had never existed; or it had and he would never find it. His father had never mentioned such a thing; certainly he would have told him about it.

There were other things to do while he was here. He would have to add more memory units to the ship's cybernetics, thus extending its range of knowledge and surrogate experience, and through this its capacity to solve more problems. He would have to examine some of the other weapons in the arsenal, become familiar with them so he could teach others their use when the time came.

He got up from his chair at the war table and went out into the hallway and down a lighted passage to his right. It sloped gently into the depths. After he had gone a quarter-mile it became level and led through an archway into a large circular room. There was a large light in the center of the high ceiling; it shone brightly, with not a trace of flicker – as it must have during the war, without fail, up to this very moment.

The floor was set with polished stones, and except for a bit of dust here and there it was still perfect, its mosaic unbroken. There were doors set every six feet apart, all around the room. They were all open. Each led into a weapons storage room; each room contained further doors which led into more rooms – and so on for many square miles. He had never been in all of them.

He chose a door at random and went in. The square room was taken up completely with shelves. The cylinder, as Myraa had described it for him, would be packed in a black protective case about a foot square. The orange star of the empire, usually reserved for uniformed soldiers, would appear in each corner.

Before him on the shelves were hundreds of handweapons, all the same type, each strapped against its packing board with a generous supply of power capsules laid out on either side of the barrel. Certainly he would never lack handweapons.

He searched through room after room, with no success.

There were chambers filled with nothing but personal screen units. Others were filled with field ration packs. Still others were filled with nothing more than uniforms. Everything seemed to be duplicated into infinity, useful to him only as replacements. The cylinder just didn't seem to exist, anywhere. He began to doubt that he would find it here at all. It had to be somewhere else.

He stopped looking for it and went to find more plug-in

shells for his computer banks. He found them in their usual place – through the sixth door in the circular room. He picked up two boxes and carried them out to the ship. There he opened the large sidelock and carried them into the control room. It seemed strange to him to have the ship open like this. He was used to it as a place of safety, and to see other light coming into it through the larger lock made him feel vulnerable.

He spent two standard hours plugging the new memory units into the computer. He had no idea of what these units contained, but he was sure that in time they might prove useful.

The thought of not finding the cylinder surrounded his consciousness, even when he tried not to think of it. It hung in the back of his mind like a sentence of doom. It could very well turn out to be just that, he thought. Again he tried to review what he knew about it. Only a few had been made, and still fewer had been 'loaded' with troops; it had been difficult to convince troops to be 'stored' in this way. In the end time had run out and the device had not come into effective use at all. If it had been used, the war might have turned out differently. Ten scout ships would have been able to invade entire worlds, landing swiftly to materialise troops for a quick takeover. The thought made his pulse beat faster. Briefly hatred welled up inside his chest, a sudden knot which passed.

Later he ate, and went on another search. Again he failed to find the cylinder.

At last he went to the small almost empty room beneath the war chamber which served as his father's tomb; once it had been his quarters. He stood there for a time, looking down at the plain black casket. Then he looked at the small military bed where his father had died, of a swift muscular infection which Gorgias had not been able to diagnose quickly enough to save him. He remembered the stillness afterward. Then he had gotten the casket from one of the storerooms. It had made a lot of noise as he had dragged it through the halls. He had put the soldier inside and sealed the enclosure. He had made the bed quickly then and left. Now he pictured his earlier self leaving the room, and he followed.

He went back to the ship, sealed all the locks, and slept for a long time. Much longer than usual.

* * *

Myraa listened. Her thoughts reached out across space-time. She touched his sleeping thoughts, but she could see clearly even from her world at the spiral's edge. She listened to all living things in the ornament which was the universe, the fragile bubble which swam in a sea of chaos, and once every eighty billion years reached a point of startling brilliance. And threw back the darkness.

She pitied his efforts, and tried to caress his spark of awareness, speak to him as a soft song. He would have to come by himself. It could not be otherwise. He could not be drawn sooner.

Gorgias' dreams spoke of treason and fear. He saw again the girl who had looked at him in the great auditorium on Wolfe IV. Her face became Myraa's and she was singing a beautiful song. He feared that at any moment she would stop singing and cry out to reveal him. As he feared he longed for her embrace. She whispered in his ear as he held her, but the words were unclear. She became small and soft in his arms, open and shaking slightly. In a moment she would be his. . . .

He woke up in a sweat. He got up and opened the sidelock and went out to stand on the concrete by the ship.

He stood and listened.

The aged lights continued to shine without a flicker; in the background he dimly heard the hum of the generators somewhere far below him. He felt as if he sensed invisible beings moving in the vast honeycomb of the base. The air smelled of dampness.

His mind conjured a din-filled base preparing for war. He heard furious shouting and harsh expletives coming from the war room. A cold shiver went up his spine, and he wished that he might have lived then, when each moment of life had been charged with meaning and resolve, and the future had been a real choice of alternatives. What a difference he might have made!

Somehow he felt that he would never find the crystal cylinder here; because it was not here. Perhaps it was on Myraa's World, in one of the old ships rusting in the blast desert, which those same ships had cut out of the land with their last gasp.

There was nothing for it but to go and look. One thing was certain. He had to leave this base, before it filled him up completely with its inertia. Somewhere below, he knew, were luxury quarters where he might live out a lifetime in comfort. Perhaps he could even carry off a few of the earthborn women to keep himself amused. If he indulged himself here, he knew that he would drift off into a waking dream, and never waken.

He turned and walked back into the ship, securing the sidelock behind himself. In the control room he sat down at his command station and checked the panel. Gradually he brought the ship up to operating power.

He wondered when he would be back here again.

8. Ends and Means

On the screen Julian Poincaré said in a low voice, 'Help me, Rafael, I like the parties I go to. It would humiliate me to be replaced at my age. Catch him soon. Submit an optimistic plan, anything to make it look like we're doing more.'

'We're doing quite a lot, Julian. We've always done a lot.'

'It's got to look like more.'

'We're ready to leave for Myraa's World,' Kurbi said.

'Fine – and on your way review everything you know, every scrap of information you have on Gorgias' history and activities to date. You can never guess what your mind might conjure up in an idle moment.'

'I'll try, Julian.'

'Have the officials on Wolfe IV been giving you any more trouble?'

'The Mayor of New Bosporus called me up face to face, and lectured to me about how Wolfe pays Earth federation taxes and is entitled to a bit of protection from lunatic renegades. He said he didn't care a hoot about the life of some composer imported by the intelligentsia for their delectation, but that he would not tolerate the ruin of his career.'

'He said that?'

Kurbi smiled. 'Not quite in those words, but almost. He then went on to read me a list of all his accomplishments until I cut him off.'

'What's his name? I mean as a point of curiosity.'

'Platon Grimm, I think. He won't be calling again. I think he wants to forget the matter as soon as possible.'

'It would be nice if we could too, speaking of careers and things.'

'As long as you're chairman of the postwar dispositions commission, I'll stay on the job. Don't worry too much, it's almost an hereditary office, isn't it?'

'Tell that to some of the young puritan militants.'

'And everyone counts on you to bring steadfast sobriety to the yearly meeting,' Kurbi said.

There was a silence between the two men. Then Poincaré's face brightened into a smile and he said, 'Maybe Gorgias will just disappear this time, forever, and live out his life in monkish seclusion?'

'Unlikely,' Kurbi said.

'What are you looking for, Raf? So what if a bunch of them escaped into the Magellanic Clouds? What if there is a colony there? I don't care if they do start another empire there, there's plenty of room for them. Come to think of it, we could never even find an empire out there if it existed, unless it was spread over thousands of worlds, and even then the odds would be against finding any one of them.'

'One thing, Julian: Herculeans are descended from Earth, and human beings have always had a wretched curiosity about their own kind. If they are there, they'll come and find us eventually.'

'Oh, I don't know, I can think of a number of people who I have no desire to ever see again.'

'I must find him,' Kurbi said.

'Do you ever think of anything else?'

'Humanity's future.'

'Now how do I explain that to the commission?'

'Has it ever come to your mind how little humankind

has accomplished in the last twenty centuries? There have been no genuine advances toward integrating the sciences; precious little in technology that is not a refinement or restyling of the past; no commanding art forms to mention. We have produced an awesome syncretism of styles and sounds and visual appearances, but nothing original; nothing that belongs to us, except the greatest war ever waged, and we're still recovering from it centuries after its end. We're a living fossil as a culture, a museum display of every period from Earth history existing on some world in the Federation; a starflung species which uses the universe, world after world, swallowing alien cultures, moving on. Oh, how I wish we would run into another interstellar species as powerful as we are, so that could take us down a few pegs, make us see ourselves. The only enemy we've been able to generate, the Herculeans, were an accident resulting from the open use of the first stardrives, and they were no better than us; unfortunately, not enough remains to be sure. . . . '

Kurbi paused. 'I'm sorry, Julian, you've had it with me up to here, haven't you?'

'Stay where you are, don't leave Wolfe. I'm coming out there myself.'

'You'll be delaying me, you know.'

'What's a few days, a week, after all the time you've put into this thing. I'll bring another ship, a big one, and it will get everyone here excited, as if we're on to something. Besides, Myraa's World is supposed to be lovely and I need a vacation.'

Kurbi nodded reluctantly. 'It won't be a vacation if we find Gorgias there, Julian.'

'Do you think we will, really?'

'Call it anything you want, but this will be it, I believe it. I'm not trying to scare you off, Julian.'

'Anyway, wait for me, Raf,' Poincaré said and broke the connection.

Maybe if we had lost the war, Kurbi thought. There was a lot in the rebarbarisation theories of history. Our enemy had been in reality our greatest friend and ally. His victory would have insured a fertile disruption of our culture, given all the individual worlds a chance to planetise the cultures, to cultivate more than the superficial differences maintained for the sake of style.

Sitting at his command station, Kurbi felt the darkness pressing in around him. He thought, the war has been over for centuries and I who never saw it feel that it was a recent thing. Somewhere the ghosts of that conflagration still raged; the gestures were still being made somewhere near the edge of his vision, and if he could only turn his head fast enough he would glimpse a huge fresco of titanic forms locked in combat, huge limbs embracing over burning worlds, yawning throats gasping for air in the flames. . . .

Captain Scott came into the control room and sat down at his right in one of the three command stations.

'We're going to wait a week,' Kurbi said, 'until Poincaré gets here with another ship.'

'What can he do that we can't do ourselves?'

Kurbi turned in his seat to look at the officer. 'And what do you think we can do for ourselves?' Kurbi made sure that his face gave no clue to what he was thinking.

Scott was silent for a moment, and then he smiled. 'Why . . . nothing, everyone knows this whole thing is a farce, a nice fat deal for you – '

'Get out!' Kurbi shouted.

Scott jumped up, shaking, and left the control room.

Kurbi settled back in his seat in front of the screen. Such a dull officer, he thought, not to have seen more in me than that. And he's been with me for a while, too. The man was dead set on what was coming to him from the service. He would carry out orders without question, without belief or conviction.

Even Gorgias had more than that inside him.

For a moment he wished that Gorgias might have a real chance to strike back at the Earth and its Federation; then he would be able to join him, help him make the difference.

Kurbi smiled, mocking himself inwardly. There was still a bit of the fool in him left over from his youth, the same fool who had chased after Grazia when she wouldn't have him, and whose life had come to nothing more than a gloomy vision of his own kind.

Poincaré was trying to cheer him up by intruding; or he was afraid that his friend Rafael might go over the deep end, and he wanted to be around to pick up the pieces. Was it too much to hope that somehow he had struck a responsive cord in Julian? In any case he would have a wit to talk things over with every day. He could be sure of that much.

He closed his eyes and tried to sleep, but it was impossible. He got up and paced around the control room, finally turning on the screen to try to find Earth among the stars. He added a coordinate grid and pinpointed the stars at a distance of fifteen light-years, wondering why Poincaré needed a week to get here. What kind of a ship was he coming in, anyway?

He sat down again, and this time was able to sleep.

9. Myraa's World

'I will do such things –
What they are yet I know not – but they shall be
The terror of the earth.'

– King Lear

He saw himself and Myraa suspended in a perfectly clear sea, she moving on her back below him, limbs open and long hair streaming freely; he a perfectly muscled body, sinewy fibers wrapped around the bones of his skeleton in a strong grip.

He pushed down to her, grasped her head with both hands and kissed her.

The outsider's view persisted. He saw himself with her, saw the rings of water moving away from the intertwined bodies. The watery plenum was filled with light.

He held a water-filled crystalline globe in his hand, holding it up against the sheet of white light which was the sky, watching the figures turning slowly in the liquid. He stood up and hurled it from him, watched as it burst on the ground. He saw the little figures holding themselves together as the water rushed away. . . .

The laser cut through the bodies on the ground. He watched hands thrust forward from a dozen torsos, grasp-

ing. His own mouth was in the dirt and he felt the beam touch his insides with pain and warm the earth under his belly.

Blink.

Drown, sink down, flee out at light into the sea mud, surface into a vise of pain.

His eyes refused to roll down from inside his head. He groped with a hundred hands into the white space, straining to see something dark. His eyes were made of polished marble set in the liquid of his head; nerves brushed gently against their stone surface, nerves of rigid ivory wire trying to pick up something to send backstage.

Blink.

Inability became a fearful mass in his stomach. He closed his eyelids. The white plenum became a dull red surface covered with capillaries. Fear became a glow reknitting the strands of his consciousness, reinforcing the matrix of his individuality, the craggy-lighting pattern of his nervous system buried deeply in his flesh, spine and brain....

He saw the whisper ship blink into normal space over Earth and rush into the planet like a toy dart, blossoming into a flash of splendor, leaving him without flesh or bone – a pattern of naked energy standing naked by itself, ready to fulfil an old promise....

He sank, passing through the soil and granite rock into the magma warmth inside the Earth, where the heat nourished his new form. Perception became direct. The sun's radiance streamed through the Earth, a standing electromagnetic-gravitational wave front.

He shrugged, shifting the Earth's crust around him, and he knew that he had filled the Earth with himself. He felt a thin whisper of atmosphere at his outer edge: weather; he felt the tidal bulge rush closely along the ocean floor, slowly shaping it, passing....

Pulse.

He tried to wake up.

Blink.

It became colder as he drained the planet of energy and was left with the light and tide of the star and moon to feed his hunger....

Blink. He knew his body was thrashing around in the sleep cubicle, eyes open, yet unable to break out of the deep sleep he had drifted into. The attack would have to run its course.

He pulsed the field of the Earth as it grew colder, moving the planet, wrinkling its skin with a whisper of his will –

– and rolled it into the sun like a ball down a smooth incline, blinking its field on and off, in a long curving path which took him into the center, shedding the Earth long before he reached it.

He filled the sun, consumed with the satisfaction that the Earth was gone; the star did not drain, continuing its output unfailingly....

He remembered living in a ship, a smaller dream world, living half awake, always failing....

Spinningspinningspinningspinning stop the enemy Earth turningturning stop.

Dead stop – millions hurled into the sky, thousands of miles across the continents; standing structures knocked flat, pressed down by a giant hand; the air seething with storm clouds and strange lights. And the sun had received the shards....

He breathed in the burning plasma gales.

The sun flickered –

– cut off for a second eons of streaming into space. In a moment the star would not be enough.

Angrily he drew himself into a concentrated mass, shaping it into –

A leaping shout of energy and light, a huge spark jumping between the stars, leaving the sun of his father's enemies to collapse into a dark pitiable thing glowing on the edge of red and black, dying.

Sirius.

Time of passage was zero, though lesser vantages would

have felt the time. He bathed in the star, his consciousness assuming its form, assimilating its rhythms and structures of energy exchange, reaching out to notice the material in orbit around the primary.

There was no one like him. . . .

He passed through the floor of his dream into a deadening sleep.

For a moment the ground was joined to the livid green sky by a two-pronged, misshapen finger of light. In the brief silence the sky became dark again and a giant moon cast its indifferent white light through a break in the clouds and was swiftly hidden by the woolly masses, the rumbling shoulders of protean night travelers moving toward dawn. The sun crouched below the world, a fiery demon ready to lash out with a scorching tongue, held back by the storm. The rain started as a whisper and fell in a rush of crystalline droplets which still held starlight in their structures. The thick, rich earth inhaled the flood, and worms came to the surface and were washed pink.

The starship looked like a rotting peach lying on the muddy plain. Its lights were bright under the overcast sky. Rusty water ran on the ground around it. Gorgias watched himself walk up the huge gulley the rains had cut in the red mud to the large open airlock.

Inside, in the main muster room, his father sat in a one-foot deep reptile tank. He wore a huge horned mask and large gloves. The creatures in the tank with him were in a panic. They writhed and leaped, leechlike worms, lizards, snakes and things with a hundred legs. His father grasped a snake by its head with his huge gloved hand, held it until its fangs dripped venom, then brought it up to the back of the next man in line to the tank, and forced the creature to bite him. The line was still very long, the looks on the naked soldiers' faces grim and resolved. When it was his turn, Gorgias stepped forward. . . .

A hammer blow struck stone.

Sirius dimmed, waking him back into the upper part of his dream. The light flowing out of the star faltered, leav-

ing the ends to rush away like a tide going out hurriedly.

He reached out to a new star, abandoning the burnt out shell. There he drew its binary companion into the main furnace, feeding on the massed power. The star flared, gobbling up its children.

The center of stars, the galactic hearth, drew him now. He went whispering between the suns, strong enough to feed on the sea of particles washing the stars, breathing the galaxy's atmosphere. He went like a beggar toward the locus of endless power, knocking over garbage cans, devouring meager scraps and the smallest sparks of life.

He hurried, compressing the forces inside himself, reaching out to the brightest stars, a thousand beacons hanging in the abyss, and making them into himself. He was rushing upward through the floors of a huge iron building made of rusty girders and floors of rotting wood, trap doors opening before his rush. . . .

He grasped a hundred stars in his net. His frontier flashed outward and came to the edge of the galaxy and stopped.

The wheel of stars with its film of gas become his skin, and he filled it up.

The galaxy breathed, pulsed.

Were there others?

Distant fears came close to him, tears moving slowly, leaving acid tracks in his cells as he tried to remember to bring himself out.

He looked out into the dark, saw the small lights beyond, felt the cold which he could not pass across.

He tried to expand at the sight of infinite emptiness, strained to reach out to those faint brushes of light, almost disintegrated in a huge sigh of stars and gases, and recovered, resting in a state of exaltation. . . .

He began to throb. The galaxy began to pulse faster and faster as he pulled its two companion clouds into his center, flaring globular clusters around the vortex across the whole spectrum of light –

Pulse.

The maelstrom of himself sucked in dust and radiation into the spiral center and spewed it out into his arms, spinning the starstorm faster, moving it in a new direction, streaming suns in its wake.

In a moment of eternity he was fleeing in a monstrous rush toward his new prey, and his light became a dark red. . . .

He thrust his fist into the sky, and his grasping fingers broke through the cardboard into a bare room with white walls and perfect corners. . . .

The universe collapsed; became a throbbing mass inside his head.

He opened his eyes and listened to the pulse in his skull. The military gray of the sleep cubicle was a disappointment after the colors of his dream-attack. He closed his eyes and pictured the superconcentrated dream-mass in his brain, the ultracompressed glow of matter which was the collapsed universe, the solid black of void around it, pressing in, containing the imminent expansion which would begin creation, extending his consciousness with it as a thin film of awareness on the edge of the balloon.

He opened his eyes again, and closed them; the vision was gone, but he kept his eyes shut. Not to sleep, but to remember in a waking dream. . . .

The ratlike creatures scurried out of the drains as the rain started to come down and the first rivulets began to run in the huge pipes. Mists passed across the thousand-foot towers of the old city; wind rushed through a million breaches whistling, became a steady whoosh, began to howl and shriek, transforming itself into a permanent howl as it reached full gale. The raindrops became swollen and heavy, spattering hammer blows against the ancient metal, stone and plastic, echoing in the canyon streets below. Girders creaked but did not fall, as if waiting for an appointed time. The drains gushed wetness in a foamy mass, washing out the dirt and rust and corpses of creatures not swift enough to have escaped.

Beneath the concrete first level of the city, Gorgias

stood next to his father in the damp maintenance office. The planet had never recovered from the war. The original population was almost gone. The forests had come back to embrace the burnt out cities; the moist earth had begun to steadily cover up, grasping all manmade artifacts in its corrosive grip.

It had been a good place to hide the whisper ship, one of a dozen such derelict worlds near the frontier of the Earth Federation. In the mornings Gorgias had left his father in the bowels of the city and had gone out into the countryside, thick with tall trees, vines and grassy clearings dotted with yellow flowers. . . .

He had come back one morning and saw that his father had shot three human scavengers in the street near the old center of government. . . .

He was asleep again, aware of the fact vaguely, afloat in a darkness teeming with run-on thoughts giving birth to dreams, turning back on themselves, rubbing against each other, ghosts bidding him to remember, furious fears driving him on. *The flapping sound of a sharp-taloned bird came up from somewhere behind him. Sharp claws dug into his neck and a ragged beak drank blood from his throat. . . .*

The darkness became merciful now, and he slept.

* * *

Myraa's World circled a G-type star ten light-years from the galaxy's rim. It was an orange-yellow star which produced vivid sunsets on the earthlike planet. There at night the stars were sparse in the sky and the Magellanic Clouds were dominant, shifting attention from the utter black gulf of intergalactic space. The planet was mostly shallow ocean, except for one large continent, half of which was in the northern hemisphere, the other half in the southern. It was four thousand miles across from north to south, and three thousand from east to west.

Below the whisper ship the water sparkled in the sunlight. Gorgias sat back and waited for the ship to reach the coordinates of Myraa's house, which was located in the northeast quadrant of the continent. Here there was no danger for him; little past to trouble him; here he could renew himself, banish the weariness which had crept into his being.

The ship was now a thousand feet above the green rolling countryside, moving east away from the tall central mountain chain which was the continent's backbone.

It lost altitude as it came in toward the house. He saw it, a lone structure dominating the hill. There were six elegant trees around the circular design; for an instant he saw the sun reflected from one of the curved panoramic windows.

Slowly the ship sat down at the bottom of the hill in back of the house, flattening the tall grass – a silver ovoid shape on a green background.

Gorgias came out the sidelock and walked up the hill to the back entrance. The sun was still high over the house before him; in a moment the house eclipsed it, leaving a bright halo around itself. Gorgias reached the top of the hill. He felt the warm breeze coming from the south. He paused before the automatic door, a step away from the distance which would trigger its open-close mechanism.

Would she greet him as before? What seemed different about this visit, he wondered. Briefly he felt like a stranger; but the feeling passed. He stepped forward and the door slid open to let him in.

* * *

'You were murmuring in your sleep last night,' she said.

'What about?' He knew she would not enter his mind. He turned over and looked out the east window. The orange sun was up, looking like a ball of hot iron. The sky was a deeper blue than he had ever seen it here before. He knew the grass on the plain below was heavy with dew. His mind's eye ran swiftly forward to the horizon where the land sloped upward to hide the rest of the world.

'Something about the edge of time. . . .'

The morning light was all over her naked body. He looked into her blue eyes and smiled. He felt the creases come into his face and he knew that his eyes were not smiling; that in fact the smile he wore was a stolen grimace, not his at all – a stolen gesture.

'What else did I say, and what do you think it means?'

'They're getting closer, they're coming here,' she said.

He looked at her long brown hair. It was all over the bed. When she stood up it would reach to her knees. Was she trying to frighten him, he wondered. 'They've never come here before,' he said.

'A hunter will try every place known to him,' she said. 'That is why they are coming here now. Your ship cannot withstand the efforts of many. No one can help you. Our starfleet has been rusting for centuries. Our dreams are dead, but your difficult thoughts swim in them. Give them up.'

He moved closer to her on the bed and ran his hand on her hip.

'No,' she said.

'I have loved you, Myraa.'

'When they find you, what will they do?'

'They want the ship. If I live they will pick my mind clean of information. But they will not have my life, and without it they will not have the ship.'

She moved away from him suddenly and leaned back on her knees like a snake rearing to strike. 'Gorgias, think!' she hissed. '*See* what you must do!'

She was three personalities in one body, one a young boy, another his great grandmother, and the third an alien once native to this world and now extinct.

After five centuries she was only Myraa.

'Reveal yourself to me, Gorgias.'

'No,' he said. He knew his answer was final for her, and she would never violate his wish. He looked at her, trying to find the young girl he had known long ago. The exterior was all a pose, he knew; sometimes she even imitated her own gesture of other days to please him. He still loved her, he thought. There was no one else of his own kind to love.

He had a sudden vision of the earthgiants around his body; and he saw his ashes being dumped over a desert as the hunters left the planet. The wind seized the ashes and dispersed them and the air was clear again.

There was only one desert on Myraa's World. It lay a hundred miles west of the central mountain range. Eight hundred years ago hundreds of half-wrecked ships had burnt the land with their last bursts of power, leaving a yellow desert where they now decayed. Earth Federation forces had not taken the effort to follow, knowing well that after the destruction of New Anatolia their enemy's power was broken.

The survivors of that grim landfall had marched away from their ships to settle the planet. Half of them died from lingering wounds; others quarreled and fought with each other; still others were hunted down for sport by visiting Earth Federation citizens, until almost none were left. As long as the prey struggled and fought back, the hunting expeditions continued; finally the survivors grew tired, refused to run and hide, and the raids stopped.

Of those who survived there were now two kinds – those with multiple-fused personalities, like Myraa, and those who had remained individuals, like himself. Although most Herculeans had been long lived, the ones like Myraa were virtually immortal; they could always become part of another mind if necessary. The young boy in Myraa had once been his brother, and had made the transfer moments before his death at the hands of a hunting party. Myraa had told him how they had cut off his head and carried it into their ship as a trophy, leaving the body to rot in the tall grass. Gorgias had never known his great grandmother. She had been a medical officer on one of the ships, and had been hunted down in the same way as his brother. She had provided a variety of sport for the hunters besides her own death. The alien mind in Myraa had been the last of his kind; he had asked to join the symbiote in exchange for a gift which he brought with him; the nature of this gift Myraa had always kept from him.

In those days Myraa had been a rescuer, a collector of souls, who hid from the hunters to snatch the doomed ones from the darkness. Now she lived in peace. There was a ban on the hunting of Herculeans. Sometimes Gorgias wondered how many she had saved, how many lived in her mind, how many she held as prisoners for all eternity?

For him, he knew, there was no safety, no rest after the war. *He* was all of his people now, the last of the old rulers of the Globular Cluster in Hercules, the most beautiful group of stars in all creation.

Wherever he went he could always be identified by his delicate short build, brown eyes and thick black hair. It had been open season on him since the beginning of his life. The earthgiants feared that he would revive somehow the power of his people; the earthgiants thought of themselves as the first human-type species, hating all others, especially if they were strong and clever, better suited to stellar life. What they could not understand in their paranoid fear was that he no longer belonged to a community, was on his own, and had refused Myraa's offer of a new way of life.

He looked at Myraa and wondered what her life was like now. She had gotten up to stand by the east window. The rays of the sun shouted their light from behind her body. Her hair looked lighter now, her tanned skin was perfect; she stretched her arms over her head and turned herself to let the warm rays bathe her body. He knew what she wanted from him.

'I fear personality fusion,' he said.

She looked at his eyes. 'You must come of your own free will.'

She turned her back on him and looked out at the countryside. Seemingly on either side of her, far away, puffy clouds came into view against the deep blue of the sky.

'I cannot judge distance,' she said, 'I can feel them coming!'

She turned to look at him; this time her face was a mask, centuries old.

He put his cheek against the sheet and looked up at her sideways.

He thought he saw her hesitate, as if she wanted to hide a thought.

'You could stand and fight,' she said.

'I will, when I find the troop cylinder. It's what I came for,' he said.

She seemed to relax. 'Go quickly.' There was a cold authority in her voice. He wished that he had her powers of mind probing and not just the keen level of intuition which the males of his race had developed. What was she hiding? He felt sure that she was hiding something from him.

He got up from the bed and slipped into his uniform. It was the same close fitting one-piece jump fabric which covered his entire form. The footwear was part of the fabric of the uniform, unlike the boots he had worn to the concert on Wolfe IV. The other difference now was that he had restored the orange star of the empire, and it stood out brightly against the solid black of the uniform.

He went to the back door and it slid open to let him out. He looked at the ship lying at the bottom of the hill; light reflected from the polished hull. He felt admiration for the ancient builders who had made it. Theirs was an older science much different from the abstractions of earthmen. Far in the past Herculeans had parted from the mainline development of earth-origin cultures. It was still the same universe but his people had abstracted differently from it, thus creating a difference, a strangeness which had led them to their bid for power. Prime forces *must* opt for their own side, he thought. There was nothing to do except try and survive in such a state of affairs.

He knew nothing of how the ship worked, except that its power source was somehow looped back on itself and could never become exhausted unless the ship were destroyed. It was slightly slower than the new solarian vessels; but it carried enough weaponry to equip a company of fighting men, and its food synthesizers could turn anything into edibles from the computer store of patterns. The ship could be captured if it did not have a head start. Opening it would be another matter. If he died it would destroy itself violently; but he would have to die close enough to the ship so that it could pick up his brain waves. He could see no way by which he could be separated from his ship. If he died it would die with him, the last of its kind.

Suddenly Myraa came through the door behind him.

'They're very near, can't you *feel* it?'

There was a rushing in his head and he thought he heard whispers in his brain, winds chasing each other, the mutterings of meat-eating homo sapiens who still had canine teeth. Somewhere, he knew, they were hunched over their instruments, hating him, Hairy bodies: he wondered how they could bear to copulate with each other.

Quickly he went down the hill to the ship.

* * *

Myraa went back inside and lay down on the bed. She waited until she could see the ship through the great window in the ceiling which was the roof of the house. She watched the ship until it became a silver speck in the blue morning sky – and vanished. She heard the wind howl outside, the result of the ship's switching into middle whisper drive while coordinate with the planet. And she knew that hunters had recorded its position and would follow instantly. The maneuver had not confused them. It was almost as if they had expected it, she thought. They would follow him closely. Then she thought to herself, but the thought was for Gorgias: *Your expected future will pass from you like the sunlight from a bright field before the sweep of shadow, your past will become the keepsake of ghosts. Then you will be mine. . . .*

10. Graveyard of Titans

Gorgias watched the screen tensely. They were right behind him in the warp, five ships this time. They were good, he thought, very good. His trick had not worked a second time. At the present pursuit rate he estimated that he had an hour before they caught up with him.

He knew how it would happen. The largest ship would come up behind him quickly in the warp, open its field effect basket and swallow his ship whole. The field would neutralise the whisper ship's drive effect and put it entirely within the field of the hunter.

The muscles and skin of his face grew tight; his lips pressed against each other. He felt a sick knot in his stomach, the fear which he could not admit as a reality. He stared into the screen, trying to decide what to do.

Suddenly his right hand moved across the board and turned off the ship's drive.

He drifted in normal space.

He counted to five, then turned the drive on again, at minimum power. The screen glowed a dull orange as a result, casting its light on his drawn features. The hunters had gone past him, and showed no sign of looking back. Knowing little of what speeds his ship was capable of, they had obviously thought that he had turned on his full drive and left the star system.

He made a quick run back to Myraa's World. There he could lose himself on the planet, at least for a time. It would be too much to expect that they would not catch on. They would miss him on their screens, turn back and make a careful sweep of near space. Then it would seem likely that he was somewhere on the surface of Myraa's World.

It would be enough time for him to find the troop cylinder in the starship graveyard.

He brought the ship in quickly through the atmosphere, leveled off at ten thousand feet, and flashed westward toward the desert in the middle of the continent, the final resting place of a once proud starship fleet.

As he came close to his destination the ship dropped to five hundred feet and continued at a slower pace over the grassland.

He saw the first of the spires – the tops of tall starships, still pointing starward. The ship dropped to one hundred feet as it crossed into the desert. Eight hundred years later the land was still dead here, a splash of yellow in the living green plains. Only near the edges was there any sign of typical desert life. Those last intermittent bursts of breath from the landfall jets of dying warships had been enough to assure that nothing would ever grow here again.

There was no sign of the returning hunters on the screen.

The whisper ship was entirely on manual now, and Gorgias eased it slowly forward between the huge ships: a rock garden, sand, discarded toys stuck into the yellow grains.

An army had died here; what was left of one. It had died of slow sickness born of nuclear power bursts, small concentrated blossoms designed to hurt the softshelled creatures inside the hard skinned warships; it had died of a lack of supplies and medical provisions; of a lack of will, broken by the sight of seething energies tearing ships apart in space, the sight of the home world sterilised into death.

The ships had been left to rust and fall apart, to slip into the ground and topple, set at precarious angles in the sand. Sand had drifted into many of the open locks: a scene of power fled, a colossal contradiction between dream and reality.

The enemy had sent no help, only sportsmen, pleasure killers nurtured by the war and not yet full enough of killing; and when that marginal interest died the survivors were left to their fate.

There were two hundred ships, useless, cold masses. Buried in one of them was the troop cylinder. It had to be here, a spark of life, of power, the men of his perished homeland, still living in a sense, waiting to be summoned.

Thirty square miles of desert. Weather and wind had blown the sterile sand into dunes, exposing stone – the bones of the planet. The greatest concentration of ships was toward the center; the disease had worked its way outward from the center, until the life of the planet had stopped it.

The whisper ship drifted slowly among the ships, a dragonfly whispering between tall blades of grass. Near the center of the graveyard it finally settled between two of the largest warships. They towered two hundred feet on either side of the silver insect on the sand.

The sun was blindingly bright when he came out the side lock. The sand under his feet was thick and gritty and filled with rock sized chunks of black carbon and fused glass. The carbon had a chalklike texture and the sand glass was multicolored, running the spectrum from deep purple to crystal clear. There were no plants or insects, only the dry terrain and the ships, mute relics of failure.

The air was hot in his lungs. He could not see between the tall ships to the flatness of the desert. Between any two ships he only saw another, between two others still another; the entire place was a vast maze of ships and sand. When he looked up the tops of the ships were lost in the glare of the sun approaching noon; only the color of the sky reminded him that he was still on Myraa's World.

He began to walk. He was close to the center of the hulks and he was confident of being able to spot the flagship; inside, he hoped, would be the prize he had to have to survive in the coming hours.

His feet sank into the sand, and he had to lift them high to make progress. He was sweating in his uniform; the air smelled of an electric burn. He had to squint in order to see. He stopped and picked up a large chunk of fused glass. It was tinted blue but entirely clear, and trapped inside was a large centipede-like creature with a small beetle still in its front pincers. He looked at the long dead scene in his hand, then let it drop back into the sand. He went on.

The flagship was taller than the ships around it. A brown-red spire, it still stood almost perfectly erect. He looked up at it and for a moment was almost sure it would fly again, that in a moment its landside engines would roar and hurl it into the sky.

The sidelock ladder was still down into the sand, and he went to it and began to climb. It was a long way up; the rungs were hot from the sand and the hull radiated its acquired heat. The sweat ran into his eyes and he had to stop and wipe his face with his sleeve.

It was immediately cooler in the open lock chamber. He climbed inside and rested in the darkness. Slowly his eyes adjusted and he looked in through the open inner lock to the control room and the cargo holds in the middle of the ship. He got up and went inside. He paused and looked out the open locks to the furnace of light which was the desert outside; then he put his foot on the first stair and slowly went up. Some of the steps still glowed with their original luminous coating.

He came out into the gloom of the first deck, where the holds were located, each one taking up a quarter of the cylinder which was the flagship, up to the second deck which was the crew's quarters. There were four doors, one for each hold.

The first was empty except for a mass of torn crates and boxes, empty of all provisions. A musty odor hung in the place.

The second hold was filled with coffins and bones of soldiers, some piled in a heap where the broken bodies had lost their flesh.

The third hold was completely empty, except for the bad air which rushed out when he slid open the huge door.

Gorgias paused, suspicious. Then he thought of possible compartments set into the walls. He began to hope. He knew he could go on to the final hold, but something held him here, told him to look in this dark place.

He went inside, his eyes wide in the gloom, and made a circuit of the walls, running his hands slowly across the curved surface until he was almost back where he started.

His hand pushed into an open space. He pushed back with the other hand to keep his balance.

They had left it open!

Or they had opened it to put something away? It would be a meaningless object to anyone who did not know what it was. A crystalline rod with a metal casing around it. It could be an ornament, especially if it were still in its case.

He began to grope around in the darkness. He felt around in the dusty chamber with both hands. Finally he touched a box. His fingers closed around one corner and he pulled it out. It *felt* like what he expected it to be, but was it? He felt for the top and tried to force it open, but it would not yield. He would have to take it outside.

Holding it with both hands he went outside the hold into the stairwell. He went down fast; his footsteps echoed. The stairs seemed to creak, to groan in a metallic way as if something were loose in the structure. He went forward to the brightness of the open lock, climbed out on to the ladder and went down the side of the ship. He jumped the last two rungs and the box fell from under his arm into the sand with a scraping sound.

He sat down in the sand to examine it. It was entirely black, with a thin white line just barely visible around the edge near the flat top. The orange emblem of the empire was almost worn away in the right corner. It was the uniform of a division – the box itself.

He pulled at the lid from two sides. It came up finally, with a hiss of gas, telling him that it had been pressure-packed and not opened since. Inside the cylinder lay in its small depression, its metal casing brightly new. He looked at it, realising at last that he had the power to stand and fight the hunters. He grasped the cylinder in his right hand and held it up to the hot sunlight. The casing was black near the top and the orange star of the empire was vivid on it, unlike the pale, faded emblem on the box. He brought the cylinder up close and looked at the terminals at the bottom where it would plug into the power sources on the tripod. He smiled.

It had been here because it had to be here. It had waited, safe all these years, until the time came when he needed it most.

He was the empire now. Myraa would have to recognise the fact. And it was a fact, of that he was sure. He looked up at the ship which towered over him as he sat in the sand, and he dreamed of a time to come when all these ships would be active again, under his command.

He felt the hot sand burning him through his uniform, and he remembered how little time there was. The hunters would be back in a few hours, a day at most.

He got up. Carefully he placed the cylinder back in its box and fitted the top on. Then as quickly as he could he began to walk back toward his ship. He held the flat box with both hands in front of him.

It had not taken long. The orange sun was only a little past noon.

11. Lesser Magellanic

When he brought the ship in over the house he saw Myraa standing in the front door, watching him. He felt it as much more than her eyes looking up at the ship; more than the magnified image of her face on the screen. He *felt* her presence near the edges of his mind, circling his awareness, not daring to enter, afraid to probe.

He landed the ship at the bottom of the hill, in back of the house as before.

He went up the hill and came in the back door to find her standing in the middle of the room, watching him, with the sunlight shining through the ceiling and all over her. Silently she turned her body in the rays. He came up close to her and looked into her expressionless face.

'They are close again,' she said.

'It won't do them any good,' he said. 'At worst they'll have to pry me out of my ship, and still the ship will not be theirs.' He looked out the west window. Wind waved the grass on the plain; the distant mountains were motionless.

'And what if I am killed in the fight?' She did not look at him as she asked the question.

There was an awkward silence between them.

She went to the bed and stretched out on the silver covering which she had put on while he was gone. It caught the afternoon sunlight and darted it into his eyes in the form of a thousand silver slivers. Her long hair lay on either side of her. He watched her as she stared through the sky window. He stood in the silence a while before he spoke.

'I found the troop cylinder,' he said.

Slowly, almost imperceptibly, the space between them seemed to become charged with an alien strangeness.

'It's only a tactical weapon,' she said without looking at him. 'If you don't win with the first blow, you'll have to supply and cover your force during retreat. Where will you retreat, Gorgias? You have never commanded a large force.'

'What can they use against me, here and now?'

He felt her impatience as a reply. Her will was a fortress; it made her immune to the universe. What did the future look like to her, he wondered. He always thought that her thoughts were one with his efforts, but now she seemed to view him with a superior attention; there was no urgency in her, no fear.

She got up from her bed. 'Come with me,' she said as she reached under the bed for a moment. He watched the curve of her back, the strong muscles in her thighs, as she squatted and then stood up.

In the center of the room a portion of the floor slid away, revealing a stairway leading under the house into the hill. The opening was a narrow rectangle; the daylight illuminated only the first ten gray steps.

Myraa went down into the hill. He started to follow when her head disappeared below ground. The lights were on when he came down the stairs after her. He saw her, far below him on the stairs, a naked figure moving slowly.

When he came to the bottom he saw a long dark hallway. He saw her again before him, a silhouette against the lighted archway far ahead.

He came out into a circular room with a low ceiling. The walls, floor and ceiling were granite, like the ship's bay at his father's base. Part of the wall and ceiling were stained, where the moisture seeped in from above, from the cold moist earth of the hill.

There was a silver plate, six feet in diameter, on the floor in front of him. It stood on a raised concentric section of concrete. The polished surface was perfect. Gorgias came up to it and looked down. His face and the stained concrete ceiling were reflected perfectly. Myraa came up to him and he watched her image join his in the mirror. Gorgias took a deep breath of the damp air and turned to face her.

'Stand on it,' she said. 'It has enough power to take you to the Lesser Magellanic Cloud and back, once. Only once. They left this link on their way out. Go and see for yourself what's left of them.' She paused. 'Then come back to me.'

The survivors! he thought.

'Hurry, you haven't much time,' she said.

The survivors. It was the only thought in his head as he stepped on to the plate. They were not just a legend, they were more than a dream. 'Have you been there?' he asked her.

'Yes.'

She must be wrong, he thought. She must have seen them a long time ago, after their arrival there at war's end, when everything must have seemed confusing. He thought of the fact of going there, and it excited him. This too, then, his people had wrought. And what else might there be! He was sure the tide was turning and inwardly he exulted.

'You must return quickly,' she said looking up at him, 'before all the power is gone. If you are stranded someone will have to go and get you by ship.'

He looked at her, heard her words, but she was far away from him, a figure and a sound at his feet. What was she, he thought, to give him orders and instructions. He felt a glow in his eyes as he looked at her. He felt a great urge to stand straight, lest he should arrive in front of his people looking inelegant.

He watched her as she moved backward toward the control box on the wall. He watched her, silent, as she opened the dark green door and pulled the switch –

– to leave him standing under an alien sky, a dark sky almost devoid of stars, except for the partial lens of the Milky way cut in half by the craggy mountain-lined horizon.

Apparently the planet was somewhere near the fringes of the Magellanic Cloud, but if it had any kind of rotation he would eventually see the stars of the cloud itself. The primary star in the sky was orange-red, and far away. It was probably the other star in the double-star system which held this world; in the morning the closer star would appear.

He stood in a grotto on the hillside. Below, the landscape was a barren plain, strewn with rocks of all shapes and sizes. The air was cold in his lungs. There was no smell of vegetation. There was a strange desert stillness in the air, no wind, not even a faint stir of breeze.

He stepped off the receiver plate. He looked down into its sky-darkness and his own faintly lit face. Then he turned and walked down the rough hillside to the plain below.

The rock floor was hard against his feet. When he had gone a ways he turned and looked back at the mountain behind the hill where the grotto hid the transporter plate. The mountain was a dark mass, part of the stygian chain of ragged mountains running to his right and left; its lower regions were now shrouded in shadow. He knew that if somehow the polished transport mirror could be tilted to catch some light, he would see its eye in the darkness, watching him – an eye whose nerves went all the way back to Myraa's World.

He turned and continued walking.

After a few minutes he saw the ship lying on its side ahead, a huge wreck with a dozen monstrous holes torn in its hull. It was lying in the shadow of the mountain behind him and could be seen only from close up. It had risen suddenly out of the darkness, a familiar design in the gray light.

He walked up to it, realising that natural conditions had not disfigured it. It had been pirated, taken apart, stripped like the carcass of some huge sea creature. He could see through its bones to the other side in one place, across the stone plain covered with darkness.

He saw the first of the skeletons lying near the nose of the wreck, uniforms still on, jaw bones set open in a frozen grimace for all time.

There was no sign of a struggle anywhere. When he went round to the other side of the ship near the nose, he saw the bone-strewn plain, a thousand skeletons or more of his race lying on the naked rock, as if one day they had all lain down to sleep and rotted away. The bones were very white where they were visible through the torn uniforms; hands and skulls were like a sprinkle of white on the dark rock. The dim star cast a dark red glow on the scene.

Death.

Defeat.

All have gone but me, he thought. There is no one left, I am the last and I have no one. He understood now why Myraa had sent him here.

It had been a plague, he was sure, and he felt sick at the dishonor of it; an alien sickness of some kind.

He pictured them as they might have been, lying there before his eyes, some still alive and calling out to each other, some answering and others silent; some might have crawled away into the darkness beyond his vision, some taken their own lives. The mountains had stood there, silent, and the stars had been blind; the flesh had rotted away and the cold wind had blown through the bones, and falling stars whispered across the sky.

So far from home: bones washed up on a foreign beach. No water to wash them clean. He wanted to rip himself apart and let his anger and hatred fill up the universe. He felt a whimpering of pity in his chest, and the bonds of his body, so strong to contain what he felt, would not let him free. He was the last twitching arm of the empire, the last gasp of an ancient will to power – a dying power. He craved rest but he knew what he would have to do, until the time when he would see the blood of earthmen spilling around him, soaking into dirt. Perhaps then he would cheat them of their victory; with a laugh his father's vow of vengeance would be fulfilled. He would not care then if the great darkness, darker than the great belly of space, swallowed him up.

A wind came up from the mountains; a faint trace of dawn showed itself in the gloom which hung over the stone plain. The darkness cracked and he saw that it was dark clouds breaking up before the morning. The wind became more urgent as it whipped at his face and hair. He turned to go, knowing that in the darkness the skeletons still had a kind of dignity; but once the shroud was gone, the harsh light of morning would make them squalid and even more pitiable.

He walked back in the huge shadow of the mountain, back up the stony hill which the wind was whipping into dust, up to the grotto and the mirror. There he paused and tried to see the ship in the faint gray light coming over the horizon. He saw its dark shape, far below, a dead behemoth which had come across the void to die here.

This world had turned toward the morning, revealing too late the stars in the main body of the cloud; they burned briefly in the sky before the sun, a million morning stars.

He turned and stepped on to the silver plate –

– into the room in the hill a universe away. The air was damp and warm in his lungs: a tomb.

12. Dialogue

Myraa was not in the room.

He went down the dark hallway and up the long stairs and found her standing by the bed. The room was in gray light, a strange gloom.

'They've put a restraining field around the hill. There are three ships on the grass outside,' she said.

Quickly he went to the back door and looked for his ship. She came up behind him and they both looked at the light in the sidelock. He laughed.

'They've left the ship inside the canopy, so we won't starve,' he said. He felt a quickening of his whole being; stress resolved his will, tightened all his nerves, sharpened his awareness. He stared at the gray murky wall of the field. It let in a feeble light, just enough to keep off the darkness.

'They can set up a power plant outside and leave it to sustain this prison forever!' she said.

'They want the ship. If I order the ship to destruct, they'll gain nothing. The explosion would throw a disrupting wave into near subspace which would damage any ship within ten light-years, and take them, us, and the whole planet with it. No, they will drop the canopy, and I will be ready with my surprise.'

'But later,' Myraa said, 'even if you win they will send

a larger force against you. Once you release your troops they cannot be restored in the cylinder.'

'I must do this,' he said. 'Later I'll worry about securing this planet. For now I can't worry – immediate plans must be a success before – '

'Give them the ship,' she said.

'No.' He went to the east window and peered into the grayness. They were waiting on the other side. He was looking forward to facing them.

'You'll kill me with you,' she said.

Although she would not say it to him, he felt the pressure from her to join *her* way of life, abandon his own, forget his father's oath, and surrender the ship to the earthgiants.

He was about to turn and ask her if she was afraid when the landscape snapped into view outside. The force canopy was down.

Three earthmen were coming up the hill in front of the house. The one in the middle held his right hand up in a gesture of truce. At their backs on the grassy plain sat three medium sized pursuit starships, three dark globes reflecting little light.

Gorgias estimated that the tallest earthman would be almost three feet taller than him. He wondered how a man could be so large and still retain any civilised grace in his movements. The size of the earthmen made them alien, clumsy beasts to be shot down as soon as possible. The sight of them made him restless and uneasy.

'They're coming to talk because they can't get what they want another way,' Gorgias said. 'They'll play the generous victors.'

'Gorgias,' she said fearfully, 'their thoughts are a blank wall, I can't see!'

'I don't depend on your way of seeing.'

But he knew that this visit was a compliment to him, a sign of respect from the hunter to a clever quarry. He was pleased.

The three earthmen came up to the transparent front

entrance and waited to be let in. Myraa spoke a word and the door slid open. Gorgias motioned for them to enter.

The tallest walked in first. The others followed and the door slid shut behind them.

The tall man was older, with dark black hair and an unchanging expression on his face: a grimace of resolve. The second man was short and stocky. He seemed older than the tall man; there were streaks of white in his bushy head of hair. His eyes were a clear blue and the expression on his face seemed a mixture of amusement and arrogance. The third man was an unarmed soldier, and Gorgias mentally dismissed him as of no importance to the meeting.

'Gorgias?' The tall man almost smiled as he asked. 'May we talk?' He spoke as if he were an old friend.

'Go ahead.' Gorgias stepped back from the three men and put his hands on his hips. He would not stand near them and have to look up at an enemy.

Myraa went to the bed and sat down on the edge. The three earthmen acted as if they did not notice her naked form.

'We want the ship, mostly,' the short man said.

'You don't expect me to just give it up?'

The tall man waved a hand at his companion to be silent.

'For a better life,' he said. 'We can offer you that.'

'I warn you now,' Gorgias said, 'the ship can defend itself without me.'

The tall earthman seemed unimpressed. The soldier went and stood by the door. The stocky older man was smiling. No one said a word. Gorgias was silent. He was sure they were trying to break his composure.

'Extermination is the policy,' Gorgias said.

'You should know that hasn't been practiced for centuries,' the tall man said.

Gorgias looked at him with contempt. 'You would humiliate me, with a trial perhaps – '

'That can be fixed,' the stocky man said.

'To take any help from you would be a humiliation,' Gorgias said.

The tall earthman seemed to consider for a moment. He said, 'My name is Kurbi, Gorgias, and I'm not your enemy. I was not part of the war, I'm trying to clean up a few things after what others did.'

What was this? What kind of words were these, what could he gain by speaking in this way? He wondered if Myraa could sense his sudden uneasiness.

'The past has a mark against us all,' Kurbi said.

'Give me back my home world.' Gorgias looked directly at him. Finally the earthman looked away and said:

'I would if I could, Gorgias. In fairness how can you ask?'

Who was he to speak to him that way? He knew he could hate the soldier standing by the door, but the tall earthman was impressive. Gorgias noticed that his uniform was devoid of markings except for the green globe of the Earth Federation. Who was this man? The whole meeting was awkward and strange, not at all like what he had expected.

'Try to consider things for yourself, Gorgias. You're only three centuries old, most of what you know of the past is secondhand – '

' – and reliable!'

'Are you sure?'

'The facts cannot be denied – the wholesale destruction of the home world, the hunting parties in the early days after the war, the looting and enslavement. All facts.'

'Agreed.'

Gorgias felt his face muscles tighten. Again the man had surprised him, had said the unexpected.

'Have you ever seen any faults in your own people, Gorgias?'

'I would be disloyal if I did.'

Kurbi looked at the floor. 'Your people were brilliant, your technology and military leadership was astonishing;

but your value systems never went beyond the pragmatic, the organisational, the thought of gain for your side above everything else. What you *could* do, you always wanted to do; what was in your power to have, you always reached for. You were the strongest, the best, the most worthy to inherit the universe, at the cost of every other intelligent race in the galaxy. By your own criterion you lost. You were not the strongest.'

Gorgias felt a trembling in his insides, a nervous twitch, the tension he would never show to the earthman.

'Who are you? You don't talk like a fighting man. Are you a coward sent to confuse me?'

'It would take a while to explain myself to you,' Kurbi said softly. 'I don't want what's left of your people to perish, that's all you need to know of me for the moment.' He looked at Gorgias. 'Can I make that clear to you?'

It was again not the expected answer. Surely this was not the hunter? But perhaps the meeting could still give him some kind of advantage.

Suddenly Kurbi came up to him and held his hands toward him in a gesture of pleading. 'Reconsider, Gorgias, this may be your last chance. Others will come who will not speak as I do. Think, just think, you too are descended from Earth stock; you carry an ancient name. Once your ancestors were the most numerous people on earth; they lived in what was known as China, Indonesia, Asia for the most part. Something of that heritage must still live in you, despite your alien culture.' He paused as Gorgias looked back at him. 'I say this, Gorgias. You must not die. Can you feel what I feel?'

'What do I have a chance for in your universe?' Gorgias asked.

'Sanity,' the stocky man said, 'happiness perhaps, a woman, a son. You've never lived with a culture around you. Your people could be born again. If that means anything to you.'

'We can help you,' Kurbi said.

'You're a doctor, a specialist of some kind,' Gorgias said.

'Yes,' Kurbi said, 'but think beyond that for a moment. Think of what your people might regain.'

Gorgias gave Myraa a glance; he was eager for her to appreciate the unmasking of the tall earthman. Her face was a blank, giving no clue as to her thoughts. He turned back to look up at Kurbi.

'My people, my people, you tell me where are my people? I have no people. What's left of them are catatonic fanatics living beyond experience. The will of my people has been gutted.' He pointed at Myraa.

Kurbi was silent.

'Get out,' Gorgias said. 'I'm tired of preaching.'

The stocky man came up and took Kurbi by the arm and led him to the door. Kurbi whispered something to him. Then the door slid open and the three earthmen stepped through.

Suddenly Gorgias wanted to shout at them, threaten, hurl obscene phrases after them, strike them all across their faces with the back of his hand, crush their temples between his hands, spend the centuries of hatred which was coiled inside him like a stainless steel snake: a tightly wound spring.

He went through the doorway after them to watch them go down the hill.

Halfway down the hill Kurbi turned for a moment and shouted, 'I'll give you an hour, Gorgias! After that I can do no more. Give yourself up, it's your only hope – ' He was silent very abruptly.

Gorgias watched them until they became small figures in front of the largest ship. In the light of afternoon the three vessels cast long shadows on the grass.

He went inside and cast himself on the bed by Myraa. She lay on her back with her feet on the floor. He ran a hand on her luxurious belly and moved over to look into her face. 'Someday, Myraa,' he said, 'they will kill all of you here and export the survivors to earth as playthings. Now you make good bait.'

She was silent, as if – as if she didn't care, it seemed to him. He hated her lack of will.

'The Earth is populated by weaklings, and they have sent a coward to preach to me. I will crush him and show them that the universe is not for weaklings.'

He rolled away from her on to his back, and his face became a drawn mask as he wrapped himself in his fears.

13. Armed

The light of early evening faded from the crystal windows as the restraining canopy came on again. Gorgias got up in the gloom and went to the back door. In the dim light he could still see his ship at the bottom of the hill, well within the confines of the canopy. Myraa was asleep in the bed. The door slid open and he went out.

He made his way down the hill, toward the light which spilled out from the open sidelock. He went up the small ladder and inside.

In the control room everything seemed to be functioning properly. He sat down in front of the screen and looked at the pseudo-images of the three hunter ships sitting on the grass outside. The fourth ship was still in orbit two hundred miles above the planet. The screen readings were weak, but they came in despite the barrier. He wondered if the strength of the canopy could be adjusted to blind him. They had not done it yet, so either they could not or they had not thought of it.

Soon now they would have to lift the field and come get him with a ground force. He was sure they could not possibly have more than a hundred fighting men in the ships. In any case they would not get the ship if by some quirk of fate he were to be killed. The computer-directed destruct cycle could not be tampered with.

But now the idea of dying seemed more remote than ever; more remote than it had ever been in his three centuries of life. It could never again be a reality.

He would be ready for them when they lifted the canopy. After he had destroyed the power of the three ships on the plain outside, the ship far above the planet would have to come down and face him; if it did not flee first, he would destroy it also, leaving as few survivors as possible. That would give them something to think about on Earth!

He thought of the boneyard in the Magellanic Cloud. He thought of the cinder which was the home world. All the ashes were his now, to remake as he saw fit. After the coming victory, the most withdrawn of his people in the galaxy would recognise him as their leader. They would come here perhaps, and he would welcome them to the new home world. Then Myraa would take her rightful place beside him, throw off the *otherness* which was hers now.

He got up and went aft to the weapons room. Kurbi had given him an hour, an hour which would be fatal to them; their own confidence would help destroy them. Perhaps when the end came Kurbi would see the irony of it.

He wondered if the tall earthman would lead the attack against him. In reality they would not be the ones to start the offensive action; he would not give them the chance.

The weapons room was actually a large walk-in closet. The light went on as he entered. On three walls hung a selection of the ancient weapons of the empire: all personal arms in the light to heavy range. In the center of the small floor space stood the tripod assembly for use with the troop cylinder. It was complete now, with the black box strapped to the side of the control panel. Gorgias looked at it for a moment, trying to fully believe in the reality of its capabilities. For a moment a fear seized him. What if it did not work? What would he do then?

He had no reason to believe that would happen. He

took the body harness off the rack and strapped it on. Then he took down a hand projector, set it for wide beam, and placed it in the sheath on his chest. Next he strung four light-diffraction bombs around his waist. The personal screen controls went on last – a small metal box which went into the straps near his heart, and was plugged into the power-gathering pack on his back. The entire rig would tap his shipboard power to give him a high intensity local screen against the mid- and high-powered laser weapons of the earthgiants. The screen could be overloaded by field weapons of permanent installation type, but he was sure they could not have one of those in their ships. His personal screen would go on and off for a microsecond each time he fired his beam projector. He was almost ready.

He picked up the tripod and folded its legs and went forward to check the screen. Nothing had changed. The gray screen still showed the smudged images of the three ships sitting on the grass. Through the distortions of subspace and the canopy around the hill, the screen image gave the sensation that some monstrous wind was raging in the real world, clouds were shutting out the sunlight to make the colorless scene, and in a moment the globes which were the three starships would begin to roll toward the hill, ultimately to smash against the bowl of the canopy.

Gorgias turned from the screen and went to the sidelock. He climbed out and looked up to the house. It was brightly lit. Myraa was up. He looked up at the enclosing dome of the canopy; its dark gray texture was almost gone, which meant that it was twilight or near dark in the world outside.

He went slowly up the hill to the house. Myraa was sitting cross-legged on the bed when he came in. He snapped the tripod open and set it down in the middle of the room.

'They won't expect me to come out like this when they lift the canopy,' he said. 'They think I'm going to make a run for it with the ship.'

As he spoke the field faded away. He turned to look out the western window. The distant mountains were dark masses on the horizon, their tops a deep violet from the rays of the star which they hid.

He turned to look through the east window. The plain below was a deep blue-green. The three starships sat in the grass. As he watched they each in turn blinked on their huge floodlights, flooding the area to the house with a stark, white electric light.

With one motion he picked up the tripod, letting its legs snap shut, and said, 'It has to be now, Myraa,' then moved toward the front door. It slid open and he went through. It slid shut behind him.

Outside he immediately turned on his protective screen, cutting off the rustle of wind and the sounds of insects on the hill. He opened the tripod and set it down in front of him, and set the sighting for past the ships. Then he took the cylinder out of its black box and plugged it into the control panel, into the round opening just below the power switch. He touched the switch and the panel lit up, indicating that it was drawing power from the whisper ship properly. There was every reason to believe that the rig would work.

He punched the distance settings and beam width; he set the beam to strike the area about three-quarters of a mile behind the three ships, where the grassland sloped gently upward. His army would be recalled to life on high ground.

Below him each ship's floodlight was an eye, fully open, watching him.

He was ready for them.

* * *

Kurbi and Poincaré looked at the house on the screen.

'What is he doing up there?'

'What can he do,' Kurbi said. He turned up the magnification on the screen until the figure of Gorgias in front of the house took up the whole frame.

'What is that thing?' Poincaré asked. 'And look at that monkey harness he's wearing.'

'I don't know,' Kurbi said.

'Look there,' Poincaré said, 'the grass around him is flattened – he's wearing a personal screen!'

'If he moves away from the house,' Kurbi said, 'I think I know how we can make him helpless.'

'Pray tell,' Poincaré said.

'Commander Kurbi,' a voice said over the three ship tie-in, 'there seems to be some activity on the east slope in back of our position. We're setting some lights on it now.'

'Give us a shot of that,' Kurbi said.

The screen switched from the figure of Gorgias to the darkness.

'Lights,' the voice on the intercom said.

The massed front of floodlight moved forward across the grass, forward up the gentle slope; the darkness seemed to retreat before it. Suddenly the light front seemed to rush eagerly forward, and Kurbi felt the pounding of his heart.

He saw the front ranks of the army waiting for them, saw the row upon row of armed troops standing in perfect formation like toys just taken from a box.

'No wonder he was so sure of himself,' Poincaré said.

Kurbi suddenly thought that his pulse was going to burst in his temples. He staggered over to the command station and sat down. There was a rushing in his ears, a monstrous whispering which every now and then seemed to turn into laughter. He looked up at the screen where the lights played over the Herculean army, which just stood there.

'How in hell, Julian, where did they come from?'

'Unless we can hold them off, we'll never find out,' Poincaré said.

* * *

Gorgias released the carrier beam by pushing the only

button on the control panel, and waited nervously until the light on the board went out, signaling that the cycle was over. The beam was not visible to his eyes. He was glad to be able to turn his screen back on. Somewhere in the air, he knew, the beam had reached out in a wide front to touch the slope, and through its bridgeway had flowed the energies of the whisper ship, enough to put life back into the bloodless templates of his army.

He peered into the darkness beyond the ships, waiting for the lights which he knew would soon be turned there. They came on and swept forward and up the gentle slope.

He saw his troops, wave upon wave of armed Herculeans, ten thousand strong, waiting for his commands.

The army stood on the grass, an orderly mass of men which he was sure would impress the earthgiants in their puny ships. Gorgias stood in front of the tripod and spoke into the communicator on the control board:

'I am the commanding officer, report!'

There was a sputtering of static before he got a reply.

' . . . General Petros Crusius he-ere . . . where are we . . . what are we to do?'

'Stand by a moment,' Gorgias said.

' . . . how goes the war, Commander . . . what was your name again, I don't think I caught it . . . '

'The war is ours to win. Your orders are to take the ships in front of you. You see the lights, don't you?'

' . . . just a moment . . . yes I see them . . . I've ordered my men to adjust their polarising lenses to cut down the glare. The ships, Commander, I don't recognise the design. Where are they from?'

'Earth Federation,' Gorgias said, 'begin to move up, now!'

' . . . are they important? Why such a large force for only three ships . . . ?'

'They are important, obey your orders!'

' . . . very well,' Crusius said.

Gorgias felt sympathy for the general. Suddenly the man had found himself in the universe again, but not knowing where or when or why. And only a moment ago for him the empire had been a reality.

Gorgias saw the front lines begin to move. Each soldier was equipped with a pulse weapon powered from a back-pack; each wore a polarising clear helmet; and although he could not see it clearly each soldier wore the orange star of the empire on his black uniform.

The front line was moving quickly.

Below him each ship had revealed the expected small laser cannon from the north pole of each sphere. Slowly the slim barrels moved up and down and back and forth, seeking the exact range of the advancing troops. Behind the first line of soldiers the second line of advance started down the slope. Gorgias looked for the slight light distortions of personal body screens. The figures remained small, spiderlike black figures.

'General Crusius, have your men turn on their body armor!'

' . . . armor? Stored forces are to be supplied later. I don't think we'll need armor against such a small number of ships.'

'What?'

' . . . we do have field lasers in the rear and on both sides of the division . . . '

'Open fire – everything! We must knock out those ship-board weapons!' What else didn't he know? But he was afraid to ask Crusius. What if the general found him out, found out that he had never commanded a force even a tenth this size?

Gorgias tried to look into the darkness behind his main force; he peered, trying to see the lasers situated on either side of the body of troops. The darkness was inscrutable, the light selective according to the wishes of those earth-giants who operated the huge floods. For a moment Gorgias felt ashamed inside his protective screen. He was safe, beyond even the sound of the coming battle.

Suddenly from the high ground darkness six field lasers lashed out at the ships.

By now the third and fourth lines of advancing men were moving down the slope. The front line was already moving across level grassland. Gorgias estimated that at least half the division was in forward motion, and still Kurbi's ships had not opened fire. All three locks were still open, but no one seemed to be coming out. What was Kurbi waiting for?

Gorgias watched the lasers lick at the hulls of the three ships. Each beam seemed a solid, perfectly straight needle of light, two for each ship on the grass.

Kurbi's lasers opened up; but now each ship was being pierced with one laser for the hull and one for each cannon on the ships.

The laser cannon on the center ship exploded in a flash of white light. The remaining two were pouring energy back at the land based Herculean cannon, but there were six of those. Too many to destroy.

Gorgias knew that in a moment the remaining lasers on Kurbi's ships would be destroyed.

He watched the great silent burst which destroyed the laser on the ship to his right, showering the vessel with a rain of glowing particles which settled around the ship, setting fire to the grass.

A moment later the cannon on the ship to his right exploded, also setting the grass around the huge ball on fire with hot debris.

They could not possibly have enough ground troops to stop him now. The hulls of all the ships were glowing red where they were transfixed by his persistent lasers; they would have to lift or his men would stand around the ships until each ship was turned to ash.

The field is mine, he thought, victory on the road back to the rebirth of his people. He turned around in the safety of his screen and saw Myraa in the window of the house, watching him.

'General Crusius, move up. Keep hitting until their hulls crack or they lift away. No prisoners.'

'Not even if they surrender?'

'That is my order.' This Crusius was obviously a man they could easily spare, which was probably why he had been stored in the cylinder. He might even be one of those sentimental types, Gorgias thought.

Below, the front lines reached the ships and the army swarmed around them. Gorgias noticed that all the locks had been closed. The high ground lasers were locked solidly on the hulls from across the field, but the metal held. They had to lift or surrender.

Gorgias decided that he would accept their surrender, then kill them to the last one. They deserved to die; and it would bolster the morale of his men.

His men. The very words conjured up a new future. Myraa's World was his, for a start. Small payment for what was rightfully his.

Rightfully his. All of the old empire was his inheritance; and more.

The entire division had moved down from the slope and was now on level ground. The front line was a little past the ships and moving toward the house. The three lasers finished burning their holes in the ship's hulls and winked off suddenly. In a moment, Gorgias was sure, Crusius would turn them to another part of each hull.

He no longer felt badly about his safe position inside the screen in front of the house. They could not have done without him.

He had commanded well.

He looked down at the ships with their closed locks and breached hulls, where the floodlights somehow continued without even a flicker.

14. The Field of Death

Gorgias turned off his screen and breathed in the night air. It was warm air, full of the smell of burnt grass and scorched flesh.

A thunder sound erupted overhead.

Gorgias looked up and saw the huge ship which had shook the ground and sky with its sonic boom. The globe was easily twice the size of one of the ships on the grass below. It was moving for a central position over the battle-field.

'... you didn't tell me they had another ship,' Crusius' voice said from the tripod speaker. 'We're opening fire.'

Out of the darkness near the horizon the laser cannon reached out swiftly to lap at the warship above the field. The air crackled with ionised gas. The large ship held its position as its hull reflected the fury of the laser whips which lashed at it.

'... I've never seen this design,' Crusius said.

Suddenly six thick beams leaped from the huge ship toward Crusius' lasers on the slope. The size of the beams surprised Gorgias; they resembled the kind which could only be fired from a permanent installation.

One by one on the dark slope Crusius' lasers blossomed into light. Gorgias felt the hill tremble under his feet.

'Bring everything we have to bear on that ship,' Gorgias said.

'Done,' Crusius said.

The army turned all its individual lasers toward the ship overhead, ten thousand pencil thin laser columns. They burned at the hull for a long time, with no visible effect. The huge vessel kept its position. Crusius was silent at the other end of the link.

'Destroy one of the smaller ships,' Gorgias said.

'I have two small field lasers in the darkness on our flanks,' Crusius said, 'besides the ones we're using. Shall I reveal them now?'

'Use them on the small ships!'

Below, one by one, the individual lasers began to fail, useless against the large ship.

' . . . where are our ships?' Crusius asked. 'If we have to fall back . . . '

But there was no good position to fall back to, Gorgias thought. Crusius' division is the only foothold I have on the whole planet. He knew he could not tell Crusius that.

From the darkness of the distant slope, from the right and left, the remaining lasers reached out to the center ship on the plain. The hull began to smoke after a few moments. Gorgias wished that he could reach out with his will and crush the ship like an eggshell.

The ship lifted from the grass.

The two beams followed it, growing longer.

It burst in a large fireball in the dark sky. Hot debris rained down on the troops.

Meanwhile, the large ship's wide beam found the two remaining field lasers; each burst with a violence that sent tons of earth into the air.

The army was retreating now, a huge black spider with a million legs.

When it reached the open plain, the giant ship turned its heavy firepower on the troop mass. Six wide beams, they moved through the Herculean soldiers like huge scythes felling wheat: forward across the greatest width of the mass, and around in the middle where the men were pressed together, unable to move.

'. . . there is nothing I can do,' Crusius said. 'Where is *our* ship support . . . surely we are part of some larger operation? Who planned this operation? My apologies, Commander . . . I do not even know your name, and I trusted my men to you . . .'

Again and again the deadly beams made their transit through the mass of men below, leaving clumps of ash and carbon for men. The motion of the beams was merciless, and Gorgias knew it would not stop until every last soldier was dead. He *felt* the hatred which ruled the lasers; he heard the cries of agony and panic, the sizzling sound of the ray. He could almost taste the ionised smell which came up from the plain.

Gorgias turned on his screen. He sat down next to the tripod on the grass. He was grateful for the sudden silence inside the screen.

'I'm sorry, Gorgias,' Kurbi said from the small speaker on the tripod. 'I couldn't find your subspace channel until now. If you don't answer now, I still won't be sure you can hear me . . . The men operating those beams are beyond my command . . . they were provoked by your destruction of the small ship . . . there's nothing I can do . . . can you hear me? . . . there's nothing I can do, you must try to understand that . . . the men responsible will be punished . . . there's nothing I can do about it . . . now . . . Gorgias . . . ?'

* * *

'He won't answer,' Kurbi said, 'if he hears me at all.' Kurbi looked at the figure of Gorgias sitting at the top of the hill. The top of the hill was brightly lit and the light played strangely through Gorgias' personal screen.

'I'm going to courtmartial the entire command complement on that big ship,' Kurbi shouted suddenly.

'You won't get away with a stunt like that,' Poincaré

said. 'Maybe I'll be on your side, but they'll replace me if I kick too much.'

The picture changed and they were looking at the plain. The ground was smoking, and as they watched the big ship which had been called down from orbit sat down in the scorched earth. For a moment it seemed that the smoke and gas would cover the globe, but the wind blew it away; again more rose up from the dark ground, but it too was blown away by the wind which seemed to be growing stronger from the west.

'If I had not brought that ship with me,' Poincaré said, 'you would have lost against him. What mercy do you think he would have shown?'

Kurbi switched the view to the hill again, where Gorgias still sat inside his bubble screen by the front entrance to the house. Poincaré reached over Kurbi's shoulder and punched a button on the panel of the control station where Kurbi sat. The hill and house disappeared under the inverted bowl of the restraining canopy.

'That's so we don't have to chase him and his ship all over the galaxy again,' he said.

'Give up now,' Kurbi said into the subspace link.

That there was a reply of any kind surprised both men. 'You still haven't got me,' Gorgias said. There was a click in the speaker. Gorgias had broken the connection.

'What do we do now?'

'Wait,' Kurbi said, 'and I want the captain of your ship here in ten minutes!'

* * *

Captain Von Leiden of the *Stardrifter*, a reserve corps ship, was a tall man, almost as tall as Kurbi; a young man who came into the control room, clicked his heels and stood at attention.

Kurbi was alone at his command station. He turned the chair around and stood up. At once he hated the man, hated him for his precision and the way he stared straight ahead, as if the human angle had long ago been taken out of life, and only he, Kurbi, didn't know it yet.

'Why the massacre, Captain?' Kurbi asked almost casually.

'That was not my impression, sir. A ship is worth any number of their kind of life.'

Kurbi was stunned inwardly. He swallowed hard and looked at the floor plates. Then he recovered and walked up to the man and looked directly at him.

'You disobeyed the order to cease fire!'

'I did not hear it.'

'It was clearly given!' Perhaps, Kurbi thought, the man had not been able to control his own men.

'I'm sorry, sir. They deserved it anyway.'

'Were you in control of your men?'

'Yes, sir!'

'Do you have any idea of who *they* were?'

'Gorgias' brigands, sir. Everyone knows that.'

'*They* were Herculean infantry.'

'How is that possible, sir?'

'Captain Von Leiden, you are under arrest for disobeying an order to cease fire!'

The stone face said, 'I didn't hear it, and the circumstances were not made clear to me.'

'It is your business to *hear*, especially in a crisis situation.'

Kurbi could tell that the man was unmoved. It was like talking to a stone wall. Kurbi had little heart left to continue. Perhaps, still, he might take Gorgias alive.

'Under arrest, dismissed,' he said to the officer. When the man had gone he went and sat down again at his command station and was silent inside, groping after the stillness of peace.

Poincaré came in almost immediately. Kurbi turned around and said, 'I know it's only a token arrest, and it will never come to trial. But damn it, Julian, I can't behave otherwise and live with myself. Ultimately, I'm responsible for all those dead outside.'

* * *

Suddenly Gorgias found himself staring into the grayness of the restraining field. He turned off his screen, and listened to the silence inside the dome of force. He stood up, picked up the now useless tripod and hurled it down the hill, where it came to rest on the grass near the gray wall of force. He turned and went back into the house.

Myraa stood in the center of the room, watching him as he came into the light of the house.

'Ten thousand lives,' she said.

He came up to her quickly and hit her across the face with the back of his hand. The force of the blow sent her reeling back. He came after her and hit her again. She fell to the floor and lay there, looking up at him, eyes wide.

'Without me they would never have lived again,' he said.

'You gave little,' she said with a hiss.

'They died in battle.'

'For an impossible future.'

He lost interest in hitting her further. She was a fool who could not be regarded as being alive at all, he thought. 'If only,' he said, 'I could have had one large ship to support them.' He turned his back on her.

'But there is no war, no home world to defend, no empire. You might have let them live.'

'I am the empire!' He spoke without looking at her, and when he turned to look at her on the floor he knew she was unmoved by his anger.

* * *

'We'll have to lift the canopy to go get him,' Poincaré said. 'Before he gets any more bright ideas.'

'It's unlikely that he could outrun us now,' Kurbi said. 'He has to surrender or fight.'

'Let's take twenty men and go get him, Raf.'

'I don't want to kill him.'

'He'd laugh if you said that to his face.'

The two men sat alone in the control room of the large warship. Captain Von Leiden was confined to quarters and Kurbi had taken command of the vessel with Poincaré. When they had come aboard earlier, Kurbi had found Von Lieden still at liberty. The two men had shouted at each other and Poincaré had to calm them down. The confrontation had shaken Kurbi visibly. He sat watching the hill which was covered by the inverted bowl-like restraining field. The floodlights made it seem metallic.

'That idea you had before,' Poincaré said, 'if we can get him to come out for a moment, we might be able to put the canopy back up and cut him off from his ship.'

Kurbi was silent. At last he said, 'I think he might still think he can hurt us. He'll come out only if he hasn't played all his tricks yet. If he has, then he won't come out when we lift the field.'

'I'll bet the fool comes out fighting when we lift the field!'

'We'll *both* lead the men,' Kurbi said. 'I don't want to kill him, or hurt the woman. This time I'll shoot the first man who disobeys an order – '

'Calm down – '

' – the authority is mine, it was given to me to use and I find it ineffective!'

'We'll do it your way, calm down. Now let's get moving. I tell you I can almost *feel* him scheming up there.'

'I'm sorry, Julian.' But the sense of hopelessness refused to pass from his mind. He said the words, tried to brighten his facial appearance; a smile would have been unimaginable.

15. Personal Battle

He came into her body seeking a kind of peace, a momentary repose. He was strong, but a few times he trembled and had to stop. She kissed him and tightened her arms around his waist and from above they looked like two swimmers floating together for a time, she below and he above. In the brightly lit room there was only the sound of their breathing mingling together.

Then in a rush she opened her mind to him and he felt *her side of it as well as his own. He felt the ache for him which she held in her belly, the spot of warmth which yearned to grow and dominate her body. It was his own now and he moved to seize it, wrest it from below and raise it high, push it through the thin threshold of ecstasy. He knew that she had entered his mind to give him this awareness, but the thought refused to seem important.*

He felt his own body responding beside hers, melting into her; he felt his awareness of himself dwindling. His self was falling into a deep well –

He was afraid that in a moment he would disintegrate, be absorbed into her. His nervous system was suddenly made of glass and was going to shatter –

He rushed into the cardboard sky, broke through, and the pleasure which was hers was his.

And his own.

* * *

In the night the stars shone down on them as they lay on the large bed under the transparent ceiling of the house. For a moment his rage was spent, and she held him as he slept. The long strands of her hair were all over both of them. Gorgias slept with his right leg hooked inside her right knee. Her left leg was bent at the knee, and her large eyes were open as she stared up at the stars.

'Gorgias, the canopy is down!'

He opened his eyes with a start and sat up. He rolled over to his side of the bed and clutched at his uniform on the floor. He stood up and stepped into it. The harness came on quickly. He checked the handweapon in its sheath and the screen controls near his heart. Then he moved swiftly to the east window and looked at the three ships below. The large warship sat a thousand yards behind the two remaining smaller craft. Around it in the glare of the floodlights he could see dark scraps of metal scattered across the plain – the remains of the destroyed Earth vessel lying on the ashes of his exterminated division. He knew now that the extra ship had been concealed by hiding one of the smaller pursuit ships inside the giant warship; he was certain the small globe was still inside it on the plain below.

As he watched, armed troops came out the lock from the big ship, two by two, until he counted twenty figures. They moved quickly, and when they were past the two smaller ships, they spread out into an advancing half moon. Halfway from the ships to the hill the line slowed slightly. With their huge clear helmets and backpads, the individuals looked stocky and machinelike holding their long hand projector laser rifles across their chests.

He could not tell the figures apart sufficiently to determine if Kurbi was leading them.

Briefly he looked back toward the ships and crew of figures moving toward the charred plain, probably to look for survivors. If General Crusius had survived they would find him now. Gorgias wondered how he would react to the news that the war had been lost centuries ago? What would he think then of his nameless Commander-In-Chief? Gorgias was angry at the thought that they might find Crusius – alive – and shame him with their lies.

He was contemptuous that they could think of taking him successfully; that they could just come up the hill and *claim* him.

His anger was a breathing thing, throbbing with his pulse, threatening to burst into rage. He could not let them reach the house. He went quickly to the front door. It slid open and he stepped through; when it had shut behind him he turned on his body screen and started down the hill. He was moving quickly and the screen flattened the grass on the slope around him as he went. At the bottom of the hill he stepped into the full glare of the floodlights. He was certain that he had surprised them.

The blades of grass on the plain were black in the harsh light coming from the ships. The sky and surrounding landscape were gone and he could see only the ships and the line of advancing soldiers in front of him. The sight of their confident step as they moved forward infuriated him further. He drew his weapon from his chest and placed a burst into the ground in front of them. There was a small explosion which left the ground smoking. The line of earthmen stopped. Gorgias felt a pride in the gesture, as if for a moment his own hatred had rushed out with the bolt to strike the ground; the rest was contained inside him, a bundle of seething energy, the one complete certainty he could count on not to desert him.

He tensed as the left side of his invisible bellshaped screen flared up. The end figure on the halfmoon of mannequins had taken a shot at him. The center figure was waving a hand at the one who had fired. Gorgias aimed his weapon and fired two bursts, one at the center figure and one at the end man. His screen winked on and off twice, the bolts leaped out at their targets, with no effect. Immediately his own screen flared up again: this time he did not fire back. One of them would be waiting, he knew, for that instant when his screen would be down.

Gorgias pressed the button on the box over his heart to increase the strength of his screen. Now he would be able to let down a small portion of it for a moment, a small window in his defenses; he was sure the earthmen did not have such a luxury built into their armor systems. He would be able to maintain the window for only a few moments, long enough to hurl his two light-scatter bombs toward them.

He hurled one bomb, then another. The window closed invisibly in the screen. It flared on two sides as more firepower was suddenly concentrated on him. The two bombs rolled in the grass ahead of him and exploded, shooting black smoke upwards and left and right. The gas rose, a curtain being pulled quickly upward. In a moment ghostly doubles of himself would appear to draw enemy fire and give him a chance to make a few kills as the earthmen lowered their screens to fire at the illusions.

They appeared. Twenty twins moving in perfect duplication of his every motion. They would be useful for only a few moments, but in that time it would be impossible to tell which of him was real and which was not.

Gorgias moved forward into the thick smoke.

When he came out on the other side he was careful to keep near the very edge of the line of darkness. The earthmen were firing at the doubles of him moving on the screen of smoke. Gorgias aimed and waited. And fired at a soldier in front of him as the other let off a burst at a ghost to the right. There was a sharp flash and the soldier was wrapped in energy, a death shroud which in a moment left him a mass of gray ash. Gorgias gripped his handweapon tightly in his hand. He held it motionless for only a moment. He turned inside his screen and fired at the left end figure in the line of earthmen. He continued to fire at irregularly spaced moments. Suddenly the end figure collapsed inside his screen and lay motionless. The line moved slightly forward, leaving him behind.

Gorgias' screen flared on two sides. In one swift motion he depressed his firing stud and swept across the half moon of figures. To his left and right the illusory force of doubles was fading as the black smoke thinned out. They still moved with his motions, but one was only a torso, another lacked a head, and still another had no arms. But he had masked his position briefly, had taken two of their lives, and wasted some of their power.

His screen was aglow now as the earthmen concentrated their full weapons force on him. He would have to retreat to his ship now. He moved backward slowly. The line of earthmen was perfectly still suddenly. They had stopped firing. He felt their gaze as they watched him. They had their rifles pointed up, but he felt the needle like force of their gaze. He was still safe inside his screen but he felt the stone weight of anxiety in his stomach. He continued moving backwards slowly. The earthgiants remained perfectly still where they stood; they cast long shadows toward him on the floodlit ground. Gorgias turned quickly to look at the house.

It was gone.

The canopy was up again. Its inverted bowl hid the entire hill. The gray surface was metallic in the harsh floodlights. The sudden fear in his mind was a fleeing thing, a whispering rush of *something* alien and frightful; the anxiety in his stomach had been a physical premonition. Now it was a cold grasping in his guts. He knew that he was cut off from the house and the ship. He was trapped inside his screen and in an hour or so the air would go bad. They would not have time to tear the screen apart; he would die and that would trigger the destruct cycle in his ship's systems.

He turned and looked at them. There were eighteen of them, standing perfectly still. He had told Kurbi that if he died the ship would be lost. He wondered if they all knew that, and that was the reason they hesitated now?

Quickly he raised his weapon in his right hand and fired at them, continuously from left to right and back, and again. They remained standing, unaffected, a half moon of tall, faceless statues. Waiting. He depressed the firing stud and held his aim. Then he heard the air rush into his ears and he saw his projector beam flicker.

His screen was gone.

He felt his will freeze, and a massive weakness invaded his limbs. Dimly he knew that they had increased the strength of the canopy over the hill to cut him off from the power of the whisper ship. Desperately he found the firing stud with his thumb but the weapon only sputtered a momentary quantum of energy and died. He let it go and it dropped to the ground in front of him. He knew where they had gotten the power to cut him off from his reception of the whisper ship's reserves – from the big warship, the same vessel which had made the difference against him before. He knew now that it could rival the monstrous amounts of power which in his experience had belonged only to the ancient whisper ship, his greatest inheritance from his father. He knew these things as trivial facts hiding behind the weakness and fear which dominated his body. He still held his right hand forward where he had held his weapon. He heard the night wind blowing over the grass. The floodlights were bright in his eyes, no longer polarised by his screen. The smell of burnt flesh and ground was in the chill air. His body shuddered. His right hand made a fist and he brought it back to clutch at the empty weapon sheath on his chest. He moved backward a few feet and stole a quick look at the canopy-enclosed hill. When he looked back to the earthgiants they had not moved. He held his empty sheath with both hands now, to keep his arms from shaking. They must not see his shaking hands. His belly shuddered and heaved in and out as if threatening to burst. His neck and spinal column were a fragile span of glass. His leg muscles were set and would not move. He opened his mouth to hurl an obscene phrase at his tormentors, but his throat was dry and soundless. He was naked before them....

The sun exploded in his face.

16. The Closed Circle

' . . . man consists of a multitude of souls, of numerous selves . . .
. . . I was living a bit of myself only . . .'
– Herman Hesse

The half moon of earthgiants became a circle around the fallen figure. Rafael Kurbi knelt beside the small, charred body. Poincaré stood next to him. Both men had taken off their clear helmets. Kurbi's was on the ground by his right knee, Poincaré held his under his arm.

Kurbi was about to touch the body, but he held back; his right hand was motionless over the corpse, his fingers only an inch or so away from the burnt flesh.

'He's dead,' Kurbi said. He looked around at his mute soldiers and he knew they would not tell him which one had fired the final burst. The polarised clear helmets had made it impossible to tell them apart. No matter, he thought, they were all guilty.

'The whisper ship has not destructed,' Poincaré said. 'The explosion if it had taken place would have ripped the canopy apart, and maybe us and everything else too.'

Kurbi turned on his knee and looked up toward the inverted bowl which still covered the hill. The grayness of the restraining field was deep, seeming to absorb the strong floodlights which bathed it. The hill looked like the bald summit of some unnatural mountain.

'Lift the canopy,' Kurbi said.

They waited until the house reappeared. Between one blink of the eye and the next the canopy was gone. The lights of the house on the hill looked almost friendly in the night.

'I'll go take a look,' Poincaré said. He was about to go but he stopped suddenly and looked at Kurbi kneeling on the ground. 'Raf, we should have cut off his power a few minutes sooner, then maybe we would not have lost any men . . . and maybe, well, a ship before and two men just now, you couldn't have stopped someone from taking a shot at him sooner or later.' But Kurbi gave no sign that he was listening. The older man sighed and went off to check out the house and the prize which was the whisper ship.

* * *

When he came back a half hour later, Kurbi was still there. He was standing now, looking down at Gorgias' remains as if he expected them at any moment to spring back to life.

'The ship is all there,' Poincaré said.

Kurbi nodded.

'One strange thing, though. It's probably nothing.'

Kurbi turned to look at him. 'What is it?'

'Well, two of the computer boys are checking the ship's computers to find out why the ship didn't follow its destruct cycle – they might have to disarm it. Anyway the computer seems to be behaving as if the destruct trigger had not been tripped – as if Gorgias were alive. I mean he told us his death would destroy the ship? I thought their technology was infallible. *This* will give it a bad name.'

'The ship is very old, you know,' Kurbi said quietly, 'a pathetic machine, disloyal in the end.' He was looking down at the blackened corpse as he spoke. 'So much bravery and resource, Julian. Why are the last ones in a line so blind, so incompetent in a special damning way?'

'I could give you a stupid answer, but I won't.'

Kurbi reached down by his side and picked up the clear helmet sitting on the darkened ground. Then he looked directly at Poincaré and said, 'When they find out what they need to know, have them move the whisper ship into the hold of your warship.' He shook his head. 'Oh, and let Von Leiden out, he has no idea of what he might have done wrong.'

'Hatred never seems to die,' Poincaré said, 'it passes on like some hereditary disease. Maybe we're not responsible, maybe it is a *disease*?'

Kurbi looked at him calmly and said quietly, 'Julian, sometimes I think you are a buffoon, do you know that?'

'I suspect it.'

'I hate you, for your hopelessness.'

'Most idealists do, but I like to think that I provide them with the conservative criticism they sorely need.'

'I think you'd better shut up,' Kurbi said.

They walked toward the huge warship. In the darkness the lighting showed it as a huge first-quarter moon sitting on the landscape.

'What about the girl, Myraa?' Kurbi asked as they walked.

'We'll have to leave her here. She didn't seem to have a part in all this. We'd have to violate our agreement with the remaining Herculeans on this world by taking her. Why, do you think she might tell us something, be a witness back on earth?'

'I agree. See that she's left alone.'

'I heard some of the men coveting her out loud – yes, I know, you'll shoot the first one that touches her. I told them that, and said that I would shoot them too, after you did. She's safe.'

'You used an obsolete word,' Kurbi said.

'Remember, I was trained in linguistics – once. I've

learned to use old terms as euphemisms.'

They came to the open lock in silence and stopped.

'They'll cheer us back on earth, Julian,' Kurbi said, 'but you know I've failed, don't you?'

Suddenly the floodlights dimmed and went off and they found themselves standing in the first hushed glow of morning. In the east the orange glow of the sun was creeping into the sky. They watched as the first rays came over the horizon to be reflected by the hulls of the three ships sitting on the plain. Long red sunlit clouds streaked the horizon and briefly hid the star.

As they went up the huge ramp that led into the open lock, Poincaré said, '*Have* you failed, Rafael? Look at the force he was able to raise against us. Surely that proves that he was not all you thought. Where did it come from? It must have been in hiding here for some time.'

'Myraa will tell us,' Kurbi said.

'What if there is another force somewhere on this planet?'

'Go and ask her. I'll be in the control room.'

'Do you ever listen to what I say? Why don't you come with me?'

'I can't – face her now, Julian.'

'You haven't failed at anything! Look, I can't even see clearly what you had in mind when you took up the hunt. It's filled up your life, become a *habit* – '

Kurbi left him standing in the open lock in the pale light of morning.

*   *   *

Poincaré came into the control room with Gorgias' tripod on his shoulder and set it down in front of Kurbi who had swiveled his seat around to look at him.

'The troops were stored in this cylinder casing, in the electrical crystalline structure of the material inside!' He handed it to Kurbi who reached up from his seat. 'We knew toward the end of the war they were working on something – but this!'

'What else did she tell you?'

'Well, she said there *is* a base which Gorgias used for a hideout, and she showed me what she said was a teleport link with the lesser Magellanic Cloud, but it's dead now, for lack of power – '

Kurbi found himself only half listening. He knew that Poincaré was excited about what he had learned. But now with Gorgias dead, he thought, I have lost all interest in what is to come. If anything –

' – she said we could dig out everything there is to know from the ship's computers. And we're welcome to the whole house here. She asked only that we drop her at her other house on the southern coast when we decide to leave. And then, Raf, her face became drawn and strange and she looked old, as if . . . she were looking into another universe . . . as if her eyes were turned inside out. She wouldn't say a word when I addressed her. She's not like any woman I've met on good old Earth. Are you well, Raf?'

Kurbi was rubbing his eyes with his hands, and when he looked up his face was pale and his eyes seemed to have sunk deeper into his skull.

'You need some sleep, Rafael.'

'You talk too much, Julian.'

'Even your sleepless brain is not so fogged that you can't see it's not a total loss. We have his ship, his base; think of the archives we'll probably find there!'

Kurbi was silent.

'You can't go on like this!'

'Hurry things up here,' Kurbi said, 'I'm weary of this place.'

'You can go,' Poincaré said softly. 'I can handle what's left to be done here.'

Kurbi sighed. 'I'll stay as long as you have to.' He looked at the tripod and the cylinder. He thought, with these things Gorgias called up the past to help him, but the past came with all its defects. When I came to hunt him his life was already an ancient thing, which had begun somewhere with groping motions, had reached several stages of mock or trial order, had become a set thing, a winding pattern which reached like a spiral from the past to the future . . . to emerge where?

Momentarily Kurbi felt a presence in himself, full of fear and anger. He felt hatred for himself. Poincaré was speaking to him, he knew, but he couldn't listen. He felt a cold pain in his stomach, and in a moment, he knew, a flood of feelings would wash over his awareness. He would not show it. Now he heard the reproaching phrase repeat itself once, twice, three times; and he knew it would go on, each word a star set in a terrifying darkness, marching toward a dawn which would never come. I am the last hunter, I might have saved him.

17. Galaxy of Minds

'The ego persists only by becoming ever more itself, in the measure in which it makes everything else itself . . . by slowly elaborating from age to age the essence and the totality of a universe deposited within . . .

. . . however large the radius traced within time and space, does the circle ever embrace anything but the perishable?

To satisfy the ultimate requirements of our action, Omega must be independent of the collapse of the forces with which evolution is woven.

Thus something in the cosmos escapes from entropy, and does so more and more. It escapes by turning back to Omega . . .

The only universe capable of containing . . . the person is an irreversibly "personaling" universe . . .'

– Teilhard de Chardin,
The Phenomenon of Man

' . . . Aristotle and the followers of Averroes believed that there was in the universe a single *nous* or intelligence, that insofar as we were intelligent, we were all one single intelligence.

– Ortega y Gasset

'Each consciousness seeks to be itself and to be all other consciousnesses without ceasing to be itself: it seeks to be God.'

– Unamuno

she spoke as seasons
mark their track in
turning autumns
golden thread

– Brian Fitch

Gorgias tried to open his eyes.

'*You must try to understand.*' Myraa's voice was soft and caressing, all around him. He couldn't open his eyes to see her.

'Where are you?'

'*Here, near you. You're safe, they cannot hurt you now, you'll know everything soon.*'

He tried to move his arms.

It felt almost – as if he didn't have any.

He tried to shout at her, but he had no throat . . . he remembered the blinding flash. He had been hit, and he knew that nothing could survive a direct hit from that kind of weapon; and his screen had been down. Yet somehow he had survived.

The ship must still be safe. Myraa and I are in the ship – in space somewhere, he thought. The pain will come when whatever she has put into me wears off. He thought of the protective gel bath sometimes used for severe burns, and he imagined his body wrapped in the soothing mass.

'*No,*' Myraa's voice said from everywhere.

'Myraa! What has happened?' Then he realised that she wasn't speaking. 'You promised never to enter my mind!'

'*There is no other way, now.*'

'What do you mean?'

She didn't answer. He tried to look about him in the

darkness, find some familiar object to tell him where he was.

Suddenly he could see.

He was in the bedroom, seemingly in the house on the hill. He felt himself get up against his will and walk to the window. Then he saw that it was not the same house. Below him he saw the white beach, foamy waves rushing gently in from the warm green ocean. The white sand was dazzling, and in front of the waves longlegged birds chased each other across the wet sand.

On the floor to his left, in the bright light of afternoon coming in the window, lay the charred, unrecognisable body of a man. He turned and walked over to it and reached down to touch it, and his hand went through the shoulder and touched the floor.

The voice from nowhere spoke, *'I show you an image from my memory, the ghost of all that was left of you. They took it with them.'*

'Myraa – ?'

He looked at his right hand. It was Myraa's.

'I could not let you die, Gorgias.' Her voice was close, so agonisingly near him. He felt as if her fingers were touching his heart, gently brushing it with her words and warm breath. He thought of the ship.

'They took the ship,' she said. *'Naturally it could not destruct while your consciousness was still near it and whole. Once the ship reaches Earth the distance between you and it will be too great to matter.'*

He looked around the room through her eyes. The ghost of his corpse had disappeared. The room was filled with light. He looked up and saw the blue sky through the skylight. Everything was so vivid, it seemed. The house was an exact duplicate of the one in the north country where he had . . . died.

He thought, she carries me inside like some toy.

He tried to scream, force his sound out of her head, but it was only a thought. He thought of the fact of being *in* her body, having the sensations of a woman –

'You let them take my body to earth! To be exhibited as a trophy!'

Again he was in darkness. Myraa's thoughts were everywhere, ministering to his fears, whispering like flies. '*I could not stop them,*' she sang, '*there was no other way to save you.*'

'Traitor!' he hurled the thought.

'*Those dreams are dead,*' she said, '*and must be put away. Let me tell you how they died on that world in the Lesser Magellanic. For a long time after the plague hit them, I heard their voices coming out of the dark, that terrible cold, as they fought each other around the ships; they tore at their vessels and at each other until they died. I managed to save a few within me, but they are not like the others. Now there are only a handful like us left. We are still descended from earth stock and very much a part of those who destroyed us.*'

He wanted to die, to rend, to tear her words away from himself, deny her presence and wrap himself in his own selfhood again. But she was everywhere around him, caressing and soothing his wounds, and he hated her for it. He almost whimpered at the thought of an eternity . . . *of this* . . . her domination of him. How could he love her now, have sons by her? How could he kill her?

He was a series of remembered moments in her being. What if she chose to forget him? Then he would fade into the chaos, disintegrate into nothingness. Die. Could he die for a time and be summoned back by her? Or would she leave him on the edge . . . ?

Somehow she was in his arms. He held her firmly beneath him. He felt her thrust up at him.

'Liar!' he hurled the thought.

'*More real than your dreams, Gorgias. But I am still yours, and there can be more, much more than this.*'

The darkness enfolded him again and only her voice was left. '*In time you will join us and have as much to say as any. Us – is only a word. Only Myraa exists, and she has many memories, much more than you can im-*

agine. You will add to her vitality and permanence.'

Abruptly there was only silence.

* * *

Ages passed and she did not speak to him. A black, three-dimensional field, a sunless, lightless solidity pressed in around him; yet he felt no sense of space or time or reality; only a hopeless dread which began in an endless past and would continue into an eternal future.

The fact of his death returned again and again to plague him, sadden him, send a quick anger through – whatever kind of being he was now. Perhaps if he waited a while, he could shake it off, throw off this strange inversion of reality, open his eyes, live. He was an insect locked in a piece of amber, motionless.

He became aware of a glow around his consciousness – almost as if he had limbs again. Then he was sure; he felt limbs. The glow turned warmer, became pain, and he felt his charred skin, knew the nerves which signaled horror to his brain. He felt his body dying, felt the blindness of its eyes, its broken insides beginning to decay. Sorrow welled up inside him but he was unable to release it. He felt his body die until his awareness of its extremities was gone, and his self had contracted to a concentrated point inside his head. That point without magnitude was all that was left of him, a dimensionless locus surrounded by infinite darkness. Anything could pass through him now, could read his most private thoughts like a roadsign.

In what seemed like a long moment, he felt the presence of the alien creature who was part of Myraa. He felt as if it were watching him with a cold curiosity. He had made love to Myraa and hence to his creature also; yet he felt grateful for the attention given him in the darkness. It gave him a sense of time. He could feel that it was a very ancient mind, older than the empire, older than earth; in this way it had survived to the present and would continue until all the mighty suns of space died and the lifeless matter and cosmic dust collapsed inward and started the entropic process all over again. He knew somehow – whence came the thought? – that this being would not die then, but its will would burst the bubble of the continuum and like some great moth take wing into the skies of some macrocreation, a universe many orders of magnitude greater than this one; and as it had survived from mind to mind in the universe he knew, so it would continue from realm to realm, immortal, an eternal voyager on an upward road into infinity. . . .

The vision held him and he wondered at it. What did this entity hope to find in the obscurity above reality, he wondered. Gorgias shouted a thought into the void. '*Who rules this mind?*' Where was the Myraa he had known? Deep inside himself, he knew, she was someone he trusted, even after what had happened to him. But what if he was really in the power of strangers, aliens, to be played with for unknown ends? What if Myraa too was lost here somewhere. Perhaps she was waiting for him in the darkness. '*Who rules here?*' He tried to think his soundless shout with all the force and intensity he could imagine.

The obscurity around him became a fluid mass; he *felt* the indeterminacy. The face of a small boy appeared before him, his brother's face. Gorgias found himself suddenly standing by the sea, and the boy had just come out of the emerald green water. His body was glistening wet; the air was fresh with the wetness of sea. '*Hello, Gorgias,*' the boy said and hugged him around the middle with slippery arms and looked up at him. '*You look so tired, Gorgias. Sit down on the sand with me and tell me where you've been. You'll stay now, won't you?*' The boy smiled at him as they walked away from the water and sat down on the white sand.

How real he is, Gorgias thought looking at the boy's radiant face. I had almost forgotten what he looked like. Then only the boy's face was left in the darkness, smiling at him as if their conversation had already taken place. '*You'll be happy with us, Gorgias,*' the boy said, '*there is such a long journey still ahead of us and we'll need you. You should have come sooner, before father died, and we might have gotten him to come too.'*

The darkness returned and again he felt the watchful presence of the alien. Gorgias became curious. Perhaps now he would find out the nature of the gift the alien had bestowed upon Myraa in order to join the personality? His interest was quickening. Perhaps he could use what he might learn?

He remembered the second time his father had brought him to Myraa's World, and how she had run across the grass to the whisper ship to greet him; how they had made love in the tall grass under the warm orange sun. The memory was strong enough to recall the feel of the warm rays on his skin. Later his father had spoken to them in the house on the hill. He had told them why all Herculeans were exiles from their native land, why he and Myraa were fated for each other; how they were the hope of the new empire which would come to be only if they *willed* it. And as his father went on speaking, he remembered, he had watched the still tree through the crystal window as it cast its proud shadow down the hillside.

Until his brother's death and her fusion with the mind of the alien, Myraa had been a playful girl – one who had laughed and secretly complained about his father's seriousness. He still loved her now, had loved her even afterwards; she had still laughed to please him, but it could not be the same. Could he still consider her as a living individual?

He heard laughter in the dark and turned to see her coming toward him across the grassy field. She wore nothing and her body was bright in the sunlight. The field was dotted with thousands of yellow flowers in full bloom, and the air was full of scents cut every now and then by the cool breeze. The sun cast a glow on the afternoon. She came near and put her arms around him and locked her legs around his waist. '*In my world nothing is ever lost,*' she whispered into his ear and her breath sent a shiver up and down his back. *'You still wear your father's long face. Don't you love me anymore?'* And another voice much like hers whispered, *'You have everything to gain.'* He embraced her back and she laughed, and he put his hands lower to hold her full hips against him more comfortably. Then she disappeared and he embraced the darkness.

* * *

Another age passed before she spoke to him again. He found himself looking through blinking eyelids at Myraa's reflection in the dark window – his reflection. The room was quiet; the eyes blinked again, and once more; no sounds came in from outside. He missed the sound of sea washing the shore, the feel of night wind on skin which had known the sun all day, the freshness of rain coming down slowly to fill up the earth.

'Hello, Gorgias,' his-her reflection said to him from the glass.

'How long has it been?'

'Three years since Kurbi left.' He saw through unblinking eyes now. Her naked reflection in the black glass sat unmoving. *'You hurt him terribly.'*

'No others have risen to plague the earthgiants?'

'None, Gorgias. You were the last.'

Her reflection was milky white in the dark window, her breasts pointed; her long hair seemed black. She sat on the silver expanse of bed with her hands folded in her lap.

He started to say something but stopped.

'You are alive,' she said.

'But not the master! How can you expect me to accept this?'

'You came from a lesser way of life.'

'Lesser – ?'

'Can a child understand what it will become?'

'How can you compare me to a child, Myraa.'

'For now you are alive, there will be more later.'

'Tell me what,' he cried to her.

'Think, Gorgias, think, all the living things that die and there is nothing for them. Little things with no intelligence that struggle and scream in all the corners of all the forests of the galaxy, and die so that others may do the same; and the others who dimly understand what is happening to them, who see the light which takes centuries to reach their eyes from beyond, in them intelligence flickers for a moment and dies as they are dragged into the darkness. They waken to awareness to find a dark universe which they cannot understand by itself, nor in its demands on them. The ways of evil are theirs: evils of disorder and failure, evils of solitude and anxiety, the evils which lie in the fact that all the good they will ever know must be expressed in work and effort and final defeat. Think of all the life, millions upon billions of sparks which fly from an anvil of life, like the sparks from a hot iron. The source is generous with them.

'This ring can be shattered, the repetition broken. Feel this peace which I give you now.'

It came slowly, a luxurious repose, an aching pleasure which might have no end. *'I give you the power of newness,'* Myraa said, *'the power to look up and through things, fall through the bottom of creation as through a thin membrane into a great vastness of warm water; now is broken the myth of reality, the bond which holds you.'*

He was lying on white sand, the beach of a curving bay; a still, warm sun shone down upon him and he stretched his weary limbs. He could not doubt it; it was real, it had to be. It would not matter. Myraa, her long brown hair wet on her bare back, splashed in the green water a hundred yards away. A small boy splashed back at her; they both seemed so small at this distance, and he could easily cover her figure with his palm. The sand was warm against his back, warmer than the orange sun high in the deeply blue sky. It was his world, his universe, and it held him deeply in itself. It seemed to glow around him and inside, a fire captured forever in a crystal; he was brother to it, a chained chaos which expressed itself as order to him only.

He remembered when as a child he had once stood on a hill looking at the forest on the other side of the small valley. The land sloped away from him gently downward, a carpet of tall rolling grass, brilliant in the yellow light of late afternoon; the shadows were sharp, the landscape crystal clear, as if someone had just turned the focus of a color chrome image. Now the insight which he had hoped for became clear in his mind; there, long ago, he had only felt it, suspected its presence in his mind – a memory, but from where? He knew the complexity of every blade of grass, every bit of leaf and bark; every insect was a world in itself, every molecule of air a wafting world; and everything passing into everything else, an infinity of layers of organisation, which seemed to glow around him and catch fire from within, and never be consumed; transparent yet mysterious, a mystery which in a moment would be revealed to him....

He had never regained that moment until now. He groped after it mentally, desperately. His mind was taken upward suddenly, swiftly, with a force which seemed to possess infinite power. He was thrust into a great lighted space, as vast as all the starry void; the light had expanded to fill the darkness of the space here. He tried to find a bit of the dark world he had left behind, anything to give him a sense of distance; but there was nothing in the lighted realm to reveal its size to him.

There seemed to be no space or time, since he could perceive everything at once; he was not conscious of being in some one place at any one moment; but his mind was used to *seeing* in the modes of space and time, as if nothing could exist if it could not be perceived in that way. Was this what Myraa had told him about, the intensity and existence which she felt always, and now wanted for him?

'*Always,*' she said within him. '*And more.*'

He thought of his age of wandering, his resolution, his

enemies; both he and they lived in a lesser world than this?

'What satisfies a human being?' Myraa asked.

'Mastery, the sense of power and accomplishment,' he said.

'These things you shall have, in their true form.'

There was a long moment of expectation, then one thing became clear to him: after mankind as a species had branched out among the stars, one branch had exterminated the other. The expansion from earth had led to dissipation, emptiness, the void that would remain after the universe had expanded away from the central core where it was born. Only by turning inward could a species and an individual gain and go on gaining despite physical expansion and division. There was a creative complexity in involution which could yield an inexhaustible power. He looked inside himself, saw the space between the suns; he drew the suns together into a densely warm super-star. It was a beginning: the total control of the underside cosmos which is the sentient self.

Hatred remained, the regret for the power he had never had. Her presence caressed him as he thought about it and reassured him. He feared her power over him, feared that she might be able to kill him, smother his awareness. He thought of *nothing*, an abyss before him. He was lodged in her as in a block of ice: dark, colorless, rigid. His eyes were wide open and the darkness was pouring into them –

'Do not seek the elegance of shadows,' she said, *'be the light.'* Again she showed him the warm sun and clear sky, the land covered by graceful leaning trees heavy with fruit; the endless summer of her world which she carried within her, its silent promise of peace and renewal. The young girl he had once known now worked a subtle magic on his memory, and he dared to remember and forget at the same time.

He heard and saw what she saw. He heard the life of

the universe, the billions upon billions of living things struggling on an upward road toward a fulfilment they would never know; intelligent races lifting themselves out of the unconscious substratum of time, reaching for the vision which fled before them. A myriad suns burst into brightness in the dark and died in an instant. He saw the ghostly visions for which empires struggled, saw them locked for ages in each other's death embrace.

He felt Myraa draw him further into herself, as if into the deeper folds of reality. Around him he began to feel the presence of *others*, a great mass of minds interlocking in the darkness; ancient minds dating from the beginning of the cosmos. Myraa held them all, and they were held by the alien mind within her; and still each mind held further minds, an infinity of minds within minds within Myraa. There were Herculeans, aliens who had survived from other universes, his brother and grandmother, Myraa herself, her thoughts radiant within his – she seemed more herself, individual, more than ever.

'*We are the universe,*' Myraa said, '*we, the interlocking matrix of minds is coextensive with the universe; we are the accumulator of dead; soul-minds escape into the matrix of minds within minds, the monadic building blocks of what on the outside is called nature – the cosmos. Physical bodies are what is visible in the world of matter of the underlying entities – visible in the same way that rocks push out from the sea. The cosmos, Gorgias, is the outward manifestation of an infinitely complex mental inwardness, a divine machine made up of minds within more minds; our radiant energy is our permanence, and the inward power of nature; tangential energy, or the normal forms of power in the physical universe, is the transient, changeable transfers of power necessary to the outward workings of the universe.*' She paused, then continued. '*We can see anything everywhere. Watch.*' In a small lighted space he saw Rafael Kurbi, the hunter, and heard his thoughts whisper across the dark light-years: thoughts of failure and despair. Gorgias was astonished.

Was this the man who had pursued him?

'His hunger will bring him back here,' Myraa said.

But for now Gorgias could not tell Kurbi that there was so much beyond the concerns of a hunter. Or a fugitive.

Then he felt a strange sense of motion, and he felt as if he were being drawn away from Myraa. He guessed that he was moving along some kind of vector axis away from the Myraan complex of minds. The time of direction was long. After a while he stopped, sensing an overwhelming power ahead. To his right and left, above and below, he sensed the presence of other vector continuums converging upon it like the spokes of a wheel. The sense of immense power at the center staggered him, humiliated him, and he knew that for the present he could go no further. He could master a part of one spoke, the loci around Myraa, but the convergent center of the omega point ahead would blind him, drive him insane.

Inexplicably he moved forward, was drawn forward; he felt all his tangential, derived energy being focused . . . by something . . . within him, becoming suddenly a radiant explosion from within. He was an instrument, just tuned.

There came a rush of thoughts in his mind. He thought, once men had believed the world was not enough; and later that it was enough: the visible cosmos was all reality: nothing beyond: the surface of a dark, cold universe which showed intelligence a stranger, an intruder, face half concealed in shadow. The loss of life on the mirrored surface seemed an intolerable loss; but now, *inside* the cosmos was a vast sea, beyond the grasping life of worlds, suns and galaxies: a divine machine which was the completion of the material realm: a mental matrix coextensive with the universe of matter: conscious: a community of love.

Gorgias saw the universe from a great distance, as a man might view an ornament hanging in a darkened room. He came up close to it and saw it resolve into island spirals, then into individual stars. The whole was wrapped in a shimmering field of force and was glowing from within, ghostly and ethereal, beautiful and alive.

He heard and felt it pulse with its cycle of birth and death. I am everywhere, he thought. I wear the mask of a stone, the gaze of a cat, the peaceful stance of a proud tree.

Skies.

A starfield.

A coiled snake.

A vein of metal in rock.

A stream.

A moon.

A winged thing.

A shadow.

A beam of light.

An insect locked in amber.

Rafael Kurbi.

Sorrow! He fell back into darkness. The underside of reality was filled with mirrors opening out into all of time and space for him to see.

As he watched and listened, Myraa sat on the bed and looked at her reflection in the crystal window, now a mirror in the night. She put her hands up to her breasts and held them. Soon, she knew, Gorgias would be ready.

Before him Gorgias saw two pools which were Myraa's eyes, but he did not go up to them and look out into the room. A creature's eyes would never again be enough for his new hunger. He knew she felt his strength inside her, a new addition to the power which would enable the entire community to burst the confines of entropy and space-time. He stretched his limbs inside hers; knew she felt his surge through the *body* which was hers. He felt an infinite power pass across his consciousness, twist and turn inside him to feed itself anew; and he knew that he was part of something which could never die.

'Myraa, Myraa!' he called to her. He stood up inside her and looked out through her eyes at himself; saw her eyes in the dark window and her smile. 'How can I love you now, Myra?' he asked.

He heard her answer, warm and welcoming, and it was his answer to himself also.

'*I have always loved you, Gorgias.*'

THE DRAGON IN THE SEA

by Frank Herbert

author of DUNE

Twenty subtugs had been lost attempting to bring back oil from the under-sea fields on the enemy's borders.

A brilliant psychologist-electronics expert is planted in the crew of the subtug *Ram* to discover the reason.

And the reason becomes terrifying reality when, miles deep in the ocean, the minds of the crew begin to crack . . .

'This is the science fiction thriller at its best. An intelligent and insidiously intriguing story.' —**Daily Mail**

'One of the few great science fiction novels of recent years.' —**New Worlds**

NEW ENGLISH LIBRARY

PIRATES OF THE ASTEROIDS

by Isaac Asimov

An ever-increasing mystery lures David Starr into a perilous journey across a galaxy to destroy a marauding band of space privateers. Twenty-five years ago these vermin had killed his parents. All his life he had waited for the moment of vengeance. Now, that moment was very near.

THE NEW ENGLISH LIBRARY

NEL BESTSELLERS